"When You Can't Depend on a Mark to Show Up to Be Taken, What's the World Coming To?"

Doc said.

"Well, by God, if he don't come to us, we can go to him," Faro said. . . .

Faro banged on the knocker several times. "Don't hear nobody coming," he said after a while.

"Somebody's home," Doc said, looking up at the parlor window, which sent a pale wash of light into the dark.

"Maybe the firedamp got 'em," Faro said vaguely. He beat another tattoo on the door, with the same lack of result.

"Okay, less go 'round back and knock on the door there," Faro said.

They moved away from Pilchard's front steps and around to the side of the massive house, feeling their way among the spiky ornamental shrubbery that lined it.

Faro was suddenly aware of a moving form in the darkness, of a chunky sound, like a maul hitting a piece of wood—and then of a sharp pain in his head, and the earth coming up to meet him. His last dim thought was that it was awfully early for a hangover to catch up with him.

Books by Zeke Masters

Published by POCKET BOOKS

#21

A ZEKE MASTERS WESTERN

DEUCES TO OPEN

PUBLISHED BY POCKET BOOKS NEW YORK

Another *Original* publication of POCKET BOOKS

POCKET BOOKS, a Simon & Schuster division of
GULF & WESTERN CORPORATION
1230 Avenue of the Americas, New York, N.Y. 10020

ISBN: 0-671-45180-4

First Pocket Books printing October, 1982

10 9 8 7 6 5 4 3 2 1

POCKET and colophon are trademarks of Simon & Schuster.

Printed in the U.S.A.

DEUCES
TO OPEN

Chapter 1

Faro looked with detached pity at the scene at the far
end of the waiting room at the junction station. By the
time the 4:10 southbound train came through—he
pulled his watch from his vest pocket and checked it:
forty minutes to go if it was on time—the two marks
would have been taken for all the loose cash they had
on them, and the mechanics would take care not to be
on the train for second-thought questions about how
the game had been run.

The pattern had been clear from the moment the
portly man in the checked suit had loudly complained
of the stretch of time before the train was due and the
absence of any nearby saloon or even lunch counter,
then suggested a little friendly poker to pass the time.
Faro had declined, but the other three travelers—a
fresh-faced youth with the look of the farm about him,
a middle-aged man who was an odds-on bet to be a
moderately prosperous merchant and a rawboned cow-

hand looking for work or amusement, whichever came first—had agreed. The merchant had persuaded the railroad clerk to let them have a piece of board, which they set up across two chairs to form a table, and they had settled in to the game.

When the portly man produced a deck of cards, the merchant exchanged glances with the others and suggested using a deck of his own. The others nodded; they were too fly, even the farm boy, to play with the cards of the man who had suggested the game. There were a lot of sharps about, and it didn't pay to take foolish chances, even in a friendly game for low stakes. The portly man good-humoredly agreed, and play commenced with the merchant as first dealer.

When the deal came to the portly man, the others watched him closely, but in fact he came out of the hand a light loser, and they seemed to relax a little. The farm boy took the modest pot and crowed with glee.

Four deals later, the range hand stiffened as he inspected the two cards he had asked for. "I'll see the two dollars an' raise . . . uh, twenty-five."

"Hey, now," the portly man protested. "Agreed this was a friendly game, two-dollar limit on bets and raises."

"Shit to that," the range hand said. "I got . . . well, hell, I say let's raise the limit. How about it?" He looked at the other players.

"Not during a hand," the portly man said firmly. "We'll play it out, then discuss it before the next deal."

The range hand cursed, shoved his two dollars into the pot and looked gloomily at his cards. Nobody saw his raise, and he laid down four aces and a trey, and scooped the money across the board. "A waste of good cards," he said sourly. "Wasn't playing with pikers, that'd of been a worthwhile pot."

"Well, hey," the farm boy said. "No call to low-rate

us like that. I won me enough so far that I don't mind taking a real chance or so with it. You game, sir?" he asked the merchant.

"I believe I'm open to a little extra hazard," the merchant said, looking coldly at the cowhand.

"If you're all set on it, I guess I'll go along," the portly man said, "though I'd sooner not. Too easy for somebody to lose more than he can afford."

"We can all look after ourselves," the range hand said, still smarting from the memory of what his four aces might have brought him.

"All right, have it the way you want it. My deal, I think."

The setup was crystal-clear to Faro. The two sharps had worked their pigeons expertly, arousing, then allaying the suspicion of the portly man, then goading the range hand into demanding a higher limit. About two deals from now, Faro calculated, the cards would fall so that the range hand and the merchant would raise to the limit of their cash in hand, and the farm boy would scoop the pot. That part of it was well-handled, but their card work had been clumsy, visible to his trained eye even at a distance. A sleeve holdout for the farm boy—the loose shirt sleeve on his right arm had twitched once as the holdout's rubber bands had tensed, sliding a card into his hand—while the portly man was making a hash of the Louisville shuffle, performing it just well enough to deceive the marks.

Not much more than amateurs, Faro thought disgustedly. Pick up some of the routines, buy themselves some gadgets from Grandine's and set up as cardsharps. Don't expect they'll last above six months before one of 'em winds up gutshot, having dealt out five aces. But it was none of his business, no more than was putting the marks wise to what they were up against.

"Makes it more interesting," the merchant said. "Win, lose or draw, it'll likely come out to a story I can tell old Polk Pilchard back in Durgin—Polk Pilchard's crazy mad for poker, always boasting about big games he's been in, though I'd guess he's heard about 'em more than he's played in 'em."

Faro rose from the bench, walked quickly across the floor and stood behind the portly man as he prepared to shuffle the cards. "Overheard you were getting into some high-stakes poker," he said. "Like to take you up on that invitation to join in."

The portly man gave him a keen glance. Faro felt fortunate to be wearing a brown woolen suit for the train journey, since the black broadcloth jacket and trousers and the ruffled white shirt, now neatly folded in his valise, would have made it pretty clear to one and all that he was a professional gambler, or an unusually sporty undertaker.

The portly man and the other players nodded, and Faro pulled a chair over to the improvised table. "Name of Blake," he said genially, though introductions had not been a feature of the game so far. "Faro Blake."

"Pharaoh," the range hand said. "Was a fellow of that name I heard a preacher talk about oncet. You called after him?"

"Near enough," Faro said. No need to go into how his mother had named him for the game her gambler lover had been addicted to.

Neither the portly man nor the farm boy showed any reaction to Faro's mention of his name. He sighed inwardly—not only amateurs, but damned ignorant amateurs at that, fresh to the trade for sure. If they weren't, they'd be winding up the business right now, suddenly finding something urgent to do elsewhere. No seasoned card mechanic knowingly tried his stuff with Faro Blake sitting in.

As the portly man shuffled and began to deal, Faro looked out the station window at the sunbaked landscape and said, "Don't look like much of a territory for a man in my line."

"What's that?" the merchant asked with uninterested politeness.

"I travel for the E. N. Grandine Company of New York City," Faro said. "Precision hardware a specialty —hey, misdeal, I guess, you sent that card right on past me to the floor."

"Sorry," the portly man muttered as Faro retrieved the fallen card and returned it to him. The others pushed their face-down cards back, and he gathered them up for another shuffle. He was a shade paler than he had been a moment before, and the hands that held the cards displayed a fine tremor. The farm boy looked at Faro with eyes that had widened enough to show a rim of white around the irises.

Figured I was right about them using Grandine's advantage tools, Faro thought. "Got a catalogue here, any of you gents interested in inspecting the line and how it might help you in your own trades."

"We're playing cards, not talking shop," the portly man said, in a husky attempt at displaying impatience.

"Might be more demand for another line of goods I handle," Faro said. "Reid's of Philadelphia, also hardware. Their best number's a little jigger they call 'My Friend,' no household complete without one. Something wrong about it, though," he went on musingly. "Demonstrated it time and time again, and I can't get no orders. Every time I show how it works, the customer ain't of no mind to buy."

The portly man and the farm boy stared like chickens

hypnotized by a snake as Faro appeared to scratch his ribs, at the same time patting the vest pocket in which the Friend—a short-barreled .38 revolver with a very efficient set of brass knuckles for a butt—nestled. If they hadn't heard of Faro Blake, they had damned well heard of Grandine's and of Reid's miniature but lethal contrivance. Come on, fellows, Faro urged silently, just fold. You ain't got the cards no more.

"Agh!" The portly man clutched his throat. "A . . . I'm . . . Lord have mercy, I'm taking one of my spells, strook with the epizootic, the way it hits me sometime." Sweat standing out on his face, he turned to the farm boy. "Lad, would you mind giving me a hand out to the street and help me find a doctor?"

"Why . . . sure, sir, of course," the open-faced youth said.

"May make you miss the train," the portly man croaked, becoming visibly more ill by the instant.

"Don't care about that, sir," the farm boy said. "The, uh, crops'll still be there, I get the next one out."

"Thank you kindly, son," the portly man said, getting waveringly to his feet. The farm boy caught him by the right elbow and picked up his own and the portly man's valises with his free hand. He steered his stricken charge from the waiting room and kicked the door shut behind them.

"Well, they saw you coming, is what it amounts to," Faro said. He and the merchant were on the south-bound train, seated next to each other and refreshing themselves from Faro's flask of bourbon as the flat landscape, fading in the afterglow of the sunset, jolted by. "You'd suspicion that plump one that set up the game, maybe, but never the hayseed. And you'd let up on the suspicioning when you seen that the plump one wasn't coming out no big winner. So when they whipsawed you into a no-limit game and fed you what looked like winning cards, and the same for the cowpoke, you and him'd have gone on raising till hell wouldn't have it, and the farm boy would of turned out to have the only kind of hand that could beat what you and the cowpoke had. Them kind of fellows do that all the time."

"Had the impression," said the merchant—Selah Barnet by name, Faro learned after the sharps had been routed, "that you, uh, people made a habit of working that way."

"Difference between a professional gambler and a sharp," Faro explained, "is that the sharps don't gamble, except on not getting caught at not gambling, if you take my meaning. You come up against me, and the fellows that work like me, and you'll likely lose, for we know the odds of the game, and the ins and outs, but you got a chance of winning anyways, if you're in a straight game. We live by playing the percentages, and knowing how the game works better than the competition does. A gambler that gets knowed for being a cheat, why, he ain't a good bet to live long, and a worse one to be able to get into play with fellows that has a taste for high stakes and the cash to back their fancy."

"See what you mean," Barnet said. "Don't expect Mr. Polk Pilchard, back home in Durgin, would care to get into a session of poker with someone he figured wasn't on the square—no, sir, for all he's so hot to be known as a big plunger."

"You got a local resident that fancies hisself as a demon poker player?" Faro asked, settling back into his seat. It was the mention of Polk Pilchard of Durgin that had moved him to break his rules of not meddling in other folks' business back in the station. Now it was time for the payoff—he could use all the information he could get about Mr. Polk Pilchard.

"Indeed we do," Barnet said. "Let me tell you about Polk Pilchard."

"Do that," Faro said, letting one part of his mind slip back to an evening a few months ago in Denver.

"Well, now," said the stringy man amiably, the night's big loser at the faro bank Faro had been running at Ed Sutton's place, "that was a good run for the money."

Faro continued folding the green felt layout and said, "Glad you think so." He placed the layout in the brass-fitted leather case that already held the dealing box and abacuslike casekeeper, and began gathering the cards and the coppering tokens.

"I know how the game works when it's run straight," the man said, "and you got the name for dealing straight. So the odds're shaded only the leastest bit your way, not above a percent or so. So all it takes is the bittiest smidgen of luck, and, why, I got me a big win. 'S why I went in so big, I had the feeling my luck was running, and it made sense to play it."

The stringy man would have done better petitioning the Congress to repeal the laws of chance, Faro considered. Counting on runs of luck made for broke players and rich—for a time, anyhow—gamblers.

"New to you, I expect, having a man drop a thousand with you in a couple of games?" the man said.

Faro snapped the case shut. "Been knowed to happen before."

"Oh," the man said, seeming a little deflated. "Say, gambling man like you, you must have been around some, seen a lot of big players and big games."

"Some."

"You ever sit in on one of them big poker games, you know, where there's a fortune in every pot, and raises in the thousands? With fellows like Hugh Lewis and so on?"

"You-Lose Lewis? Sure, played with him, both just him and me and with a bunch of high rollers. Yeah, some of them pots was a long way from the slim side."

The man looked at him with wistful interest. "Since you're closed up for the night, buy you a drink?"

"Good of you," Faro said, "seeing's you've paid for a good many months' drinking for me already tonight. Sure."

At the bar, the stringy man drew from Faro reminiscences of his encounters with some of the legends of the gambling world—not the professionals, but the amateur gamesters and spectacular bettors.

"So this Gates," Faro said, nicely relaxed as he worked on his third tumbler of bourbon, "a man that'd made hisself a bundle selling barbwire, and didn't give a damn whether he lost or won it, kind of betting fool he was—still is—anyhow, I was with him and some fellows once in a barroom in maybe Houston. And while as we was there, it come on a rainstorm, and the front windows was all over raindrops. And that Gates, he pointed out two drops that was near the top of the pane, and got bets going which one of 'em'd get to the bottom first, or not dry up before as it got there."

"Bet-a-Million Gates," the stringy man said reverently.

Faro shrugged. "They call him that, I guess, but as I recollect he had under a thousand riding that time. Seven-fifty, I think it was. Didn't matter, 'cause all bets got called off."

"How come?" the stringy man said.

"Everybody was crowded close to the window, and one of the fellows that had bet on the raindrop Gates had bet against was saw to bring his cigar close to the glass behind where Gates's drop was, so as to heat it up and dry it out, so's it wasn't a fair bet."

"What'd they do to him?" the stringy man asked.

"Nothing," Faro said. "They just saw to it that the thing got knowed, and he wasn't welcome in that crowd no more."

"Damn fool," the man said. "A man's privileged to be accepted by that kind of folks, and he throws it away like that. To be on friendly terms with Bet-a-Million Gates, You-Lose Lewis and them, my, that must be something."

His tone was longing, and Faro said, "Don't take much beyond a taste for gambling heavy and the cash to back it. You seem to have got the one, way you went at my game back there, and it didn't seem to faze you, so I expect you got the other."

"Well, yeah, I am fixed well enough," the man said. "But . . ." He hesitated. "The thing is, you got to go where them fellows are, d'you see?"

"Could be about anyplace," Faro said. "Frisco sometimes, sometimes Santone, St. Louis, Chicago, Saratoga, New York—any kind of big town where there's gambling, some of them'll be showing up before long, and no problems about taking in the stranger in their midsts, so long's he's got the gelt and the spirit for it, and maybe washes once every week or so."

The man sighed. "That's it, the traveling."

"The cars make you sick?"

The man shook his head. "No . . . well, it sounds foolish, but it's my luck. It don't travel."

Faro looked at him over the rim of his glass. The man seemed to take it as a question and went on. "Like I said, it sounds foolish, but it's the God's truth. First and best luck I ever had, that made me a rich man, that was back where I'm living now, a dozen or so years back. And the luck's held—whatever I put my hands to, it prospers, and I expect I got a corner on about half the money in town, one way and another. But as soon as I get away from there, the luck starts fading. I went to St. Louis once, and was in a train wreck, and a boiler explosion on a riverboat, and got robbed, and caught a dose of the clap, and lost most of the money I had with me in two nights' gambling. I tried it a couple more times, and saw that the further I got from home, the worse it was. Worked it out that Denver's about as far as I can come without getting hit too bad. All's happened so far here, this time, is dropping that thousand to you tonight, and a case of the squitters from something I et at the hotel. Worth it for the fun, so long's it doesn't get any worse."

The man sighed again. "So I don't expect I'll ever get in with them high rollers, much as it'd pleasure me to do that. Was I to get into a big game with them in a place in San Francisco or New York City, say, expect it'd burn down with me in it. And it's a sure bet Gates or Lewis or any of them isn't going to be passing through Durgin, Arizona Territory, where I could take 'em on with my luck holding."

Faro was fascinated. Most gamblers, professional and amateur, had their quirky obsessions about luck. Some had lucky pieces, some had lucky items of clothing (as these, to preserve their power, had to be worn constantly and never washed, men of that persuasion tended to be less and less popular at the tables as time wore on; Lucky Drawers Goulart had been banned from play years ago) and others trusted to an interior feeling that told them when their luck was running. Faro's opinion was that gamblers made their own luck, knowing the game and its odds and, from years of experience and sharpened observation, how to read opposing players. Luck was just a matter of being a hell of a lot better at it than the other fellow. Of course, craps was a different matter; everyone knew that when you were on a run, you could feel it, and had best keep with it.

But this was by a long way the oddest bonnet bee about luck he had ever come across, although it made about as much sense as any of the others.

"Each mile or what you go away from this Durgin, your luck starts fading?" he asked.

The man nodded. "About fifty miles out on the train, it commences to rattle to shake your bones loose, and I get a faceful of soot from the stack." Pretty much what happens to most train riders, Faro thought. "Two hundred miles away, and I'm a sure thing for a sprained finger at least, and nothing I want to eat on the bill of fare wherever I'm at. And then it gets worse from there on."

It seemed to Faro that a man who was convinced he was unlucky would be, and he began to look forward to the stringy man's return to his table tomorrow evening.

The stringy man rose and sighed yet again. "A pleasure talking to you," he said mournfully. "Won't be seeing you again, not here, anyhow. I'm on the train in the morning back to Durgin, best get away before the luck curdles on me. Right now, it's no more than souring some. You ever find yourself in Durgin, you look me up and we'll have ourselves the hottest poker game you can handle—when I'm where my luck's at, there's no holding me, I can tell you, and so I could tell Gates or Lewis if they was to come by. Just ask around for Polk Pilchard."

In the ensuing months, the memory of the eccentric Pilchard had floated to the top of Faro's consciousness from time to time, but mainly as a prime oddity. He mentioned him to You-Lose Lewis during a game in Houston, and Lewis grunted. "Be a pleasure to play a man like that, though I think it'd be like shooting fish in a barrel. Seems to me that he's operating on a mixture of vanity and superstition that'll blow his boilers or burn out his firebox. He ever nerves himself to travel again, steer him my way, huh? Hey, Ernie puts out a good spread, doesn't he?" Lewis reached for one of the opulent ham sandwiches that Ernie Osborne, who had organized the game, had set out for the major gamblers he had attracted. "Win or lose," Lewis went on a little indistinctly as he chewed, "you get a good feed and all the booze you want. Worth the trip in itself, so it is."

Lewis's comment planted the seed of an idea in Faro's brain. In a few days it had sprouted, grown and flowered; its first fruit was the purchase of a train ticket, or rather a concertina—a folded series of tickets, several lines being involved—to Durgin, Arizona Territory.

He had planned to reconnoiter Pilchard after getting to Durgin, but the chance of acquiring advance information from Barnet had been too good to pass up, even if it meant queering the game for a couple of colleagues. After all, if they were that clumsy at it, they didn't rate being in the trade, even the dirty end of it. Looking at it one way, he'd done the portly man and the farm boy a considerable favor, though he doubted they'd thank him for it.

Chapter 2

"Well, Mr. Polk Pilchard is about the biggest man in Durgin," Barnet said, priming himself with another swig from Faro's flask. "Richest, anyhow, and with a finger in most pies there are there. But he's not well-liked."

Faro could see that the stringy eccentric he had encountered in Denver wasn't the sort to attract a large circle of friends, but it was no part of his policy to betray any previous acquaintance with Pilchard, not just now. In his experience, information was offered freely to the ignorant, and sometimes pressed on them. But when a man knew something about a topic, the people he questioned were too often likely to wonder just why it was he wanted to know more. "How come?" he asked.

"Well, he kind of thinks he owns the place. And it doesn't make it any easier to take that he's not far off being right about that. No denying, it was Polk Pil-

chard's luck that made Durgin what it is today, for
better, worse and sideways."

Faro chewed a shoetongue-and-cardboard sandwich
that the candy butcher had sold him as ham on white
bread, moistening it with sips of bourbon, as Barnet
explained about Pilchard's luck and its influence on
Durgin.

"Prospectors they were, him and his partner, back
about the end of the War, and they came to Durgin,
which wasn't then much more than a trading post where
a couple of stage roads crossed. And they started
digging in the hills around there, and they hit it lucky.
Gold till hell wouldn't have it, it seemed like. Well, sir,
Durgin just boomed after that, everybody coming in to
stake out claims, and the people that came in to trade
with them and sell them stuff—that was when I got
there, dry goods, provisions and my Matilda doing
laundry for those that wanted it, which wasn't much of
a strain on her. Anyhow, within a year, Durgin was a
real town, not a wide place in the road. With the money
coming out of the mine and Pilchard and his partner
spending it, and the wages the miners brought in, why,
it looked as if it'd go on forever."

But the Good Indian mine—Pilchard and his partner
had not only had to establish their claim with the
Territorial government but uphold it against the resent-
ment of a few Apaches, with fatal results for the
attackers—had pinched out after two years, with further drilling and blasting revealing nothing but barren
rock.

Pilchard's partner, a man named McTeague, had left
the operation of the mine to Pilchard and gone to
California to go into a variety of businesses, content to
take his half-share of the proceeds to finance these.

"Here is where Polk Pilchard got lucky again,"
Barnet said, "though there's no denying there's some-

thing kind of shameful about it. Put it to this McTeague that there was a big vein spotted, but that it'd need a hell of a lot of money to get at it, and it'd be a while before any payoff, and could McTeague come through with enough to pay for it? Well, old Polk played him just right—McTeague sent back word that he wouldn't put up the cash for a partnership enterprise if Polk couldn't go at least halves on it, and suggested that Polk sell out to him and let him get on with it and keep the profits for himself. Polk hemmed and hawed some for a couple of weeks, then gave in. And so this McTeague got lumbered with a worthless hole in the ground, and Polk came out richer than ever. Give him his due, he's put what money he's not sitting on into Durgin, which is why it didn't dry up and blow away after the Good Indian shut down. He got the railroad to come in, and he's invested in most of the important businesses in town, and, what with that, and the ranching and so on that's grown up around there, we're doing pretty well. But it sits a little uneasy on us that Polk Pilchard got a good bit of his pile by what amounts to fraud, and we're benefiting from it—and worse, that Polk Pilchard figures he can be the big mogul, with everybody else expected to jump when he says 'frog.' "

Faro had about as much interest in Polk Pilchard's past as in the social organization of a prairie dog colony, maybe less. "You mentioned he was a poker fiend," he said.

"His passion," Barnet answered. "He gets the *Police Gazette* sent in special, reads everything in there about the big gamblers and their doings, and shows up most nights to sit in on whatever games are going. And he's always grousing about how the play there isn't up to what the big fellows get into, no no-limits stuff. Well, it stands to reason, nobody around can afford to get into a game like that with Polk Pilchard. You lose, you're wiped out. You win, you've got Polk Pilchard down on you, figuring you've not played square or somehow spoiled his luck, and likely he's holding one of your notes that he can call in at any time. So he doesn't get much amusement in Durgin, nor yet the kind of respect he craves, and, for some reason, he doesn't seem to care to travel to where he might get that."

Evidently Pilchard had not talked as candidly about his theory of his luck being tied to Durgin to his fellow-townsmen as he had in Denver. The information Faro had gathered was not extensive, but it buttressed his decision to travel to Durgin.

"Interesting fellow," he said politely. "Now, a thing I was wondering about this Durgin place. I got me a notion to stay over there awhile, but I'm not looking to lay out for an expensive hotel room, assuming you got such there. You happen to know of a respectable boardinghouse, where the food's not burned and they don't think canned tomatoes is the highest-class dish there is?" Faro was at the moment unusually solvent, but his plans for Polk Pilchard called for having all available funds ready for the good work and not tied up in lodging costs and obligations. A man could only sleep so hard and eat so much, and it didn't matter much where he did both.

"Mrs. Pyle's," Barnet said without hesitation. "Territory Street, off Front, about five blocks from the station. As good food as anywhere in town, and as good company, a lot of the inmates being passing through, which makes them more of a novelty than the folks who live in Durgin all the time. A hell of a lot better value for the money than the Butler House Hotel, that's gussied up to attract the carriage trade that's never showed up, and charges according."

As Faro composed himself for sleep, wriggling his bottom until it found an almost comfortable adjustment to the horsehair seat, he mentally rehearsed his plans for Polk Pilchard. Ernie Osborne or Big Jim McGaha would have headquartered at the Butler House, if they were working out what he had in mind. But the whole idea was to have Polk Pilchard be the McGaha or Osborne for this setup. . . .

"Raoof Rggn!" the conductor bawled from the end of the car.

From the fact that Barnet, crumpled and unshaven after the night's ride—as Faro assumed he was himself —stood and reached down his valise from the luggage rack, Faro was able to interpret the cry as "All off for Durgin!" and secured his valise and the leather "tool case" that had been with him over the last two decades.

Once off the train, Barnet eyed Faro curiously. "Seems to me you might have some plans for Mr. Polk Pilchard," he said, "taking into account his interests and your line of work."

"Well," Faro said, "I wouldn't—"

"Whatever, good luck to you," Barnet said. "If you can give him something to think about with a square game, fine. Was I in your place, I wouldn't mind bending things a little to see the results came out to gratify me and not Polk Pilchard. He's had something coming to him for a long time. Ma Pyle's is up ahead to just after the livery, and then on your left. Enjoyable talking to you, and thanks for keeping me from getting taken by those two back there."

He went off in the opposite direction to the one he had indicated to Faro, who now lit a cheroot and surveyed the town he had come to, as much of it as could be seen in the midmorning light from where he stood.

Three blocks seemed to make up the central section

of Durgin, Arizona Territory. They contained the bank, four saloons, various mercantile establishments, a laundry, a print shop and newspaper office, and the Butler House Hotel, soaring a full three stories above the caked dust of the street. A straggle of houses and shacks marked the length of Front Street and the thoroughfares that intersected it. Just on the edge, Faro considered. There was enough evidence of prosperity to show that the place wasn't failing, but no indication of future growth. Durgin appeared to have become about what it was going to be for a long time, with no real changes for better or worse in sight, as far as he could tell. There was no evidence of recent construction, no piles of lumber in the several vacant lots to indicate expansion on the way. If Barnet was right, Polk Pilchard had both helped create Durgin the way it was now and was keeping it from being anything else for a long time.

The train screamed its intention to depart, and Faro glanced behind him. The last of a load of crates was being off-loaded from the baggage car just as the locomotive's driving wheels began their first painfully slow rotation. The crates were unusual in shape, about five feet long by three high, but no more than half a foot wide; there seemed to be about a dozen of them. He wondered what the hell they might be, and if Polk Pilchard had anything to do with them, then dismissed them from his mind as he turned up Front Street toward the livery stable and the side street that led to Mrs. Pyle's.

"Sorry Major Mordaunt isn't here, Mr. Blake," Mrs. Pyle said from where she presided at the head of the table at which her boarders were taking their lunch. "Always a good talker, the major, with stories of where he's been and what he's done. And likely he'd admire to hear of some of the things you've run acrost in your travels."

Holly O'Devie, seated across from Faro, speared two boiled potatoes from their platter and set them on her plate, drew the gravy boat to her and ladled out a generous quantity, and treated herself to a helping of slaw, leaning over the table and stretching according to accepted boardinghouse etiquette. He had been introduced to the other half-dozen boarders present, but only Holly's name had stuck with him. Her appearance alone would have guaranteed that—a trim figure that flared nicely above and below the waist, creamy skin, jet curls and matching eyes with a deep fire in their depths, like black opals. A prime looker, for sure—but the way she was digging into the lunch put her in the truly memorable class of eaters.

"Major Mordaunt," Mrs. Pyle went on, "is presently down at the railroad freight office taking delivery of a new consignment that come in on the morning train."

"Would that be a bunch of flat-style crates that was left on the platform?" Faro asked. "I seen them and wondered what was in them."

"You pass the meat, please?" Holly O'Devie said. Faro saw that the platter of sliced steak was just beyond her reach and slid it to her. She forked two slices onto her plate, making, according to his rough calculations, not far short of a half-pound of meat for the sitting. He made a mental note to watch her at the next meals they shared and see if she kept up the rate of consumption. If she did, it was hard to see how she kept slim where she was slim and avoided ballooning where she wasn't. The lunch she had taken in would have held a farmhand during haying time, and a pretty big farmhand at that.

"Yes, those'd be the major's new consignment,"

Mrs. Pyle said. "Expecting them, he's been for a week or so—a dozen bicycles, knocked down for shipping."

"Bicycles I seen," Faro said, "wouldn't fit into them crates. There's an almighty big wheel in the front and then a dinky one behind. Must of been something else."

Mrs. Pyle shook her head. "These are the latest thing, like the major told us," she said. "Front and back wheels the same size, and the whole driven by a chain that you work with your feet. The major says he aims to bring Durgin into the twentieth century twenty years or so ahead of time by putting us on wheels."

Holly O'Devie lightened the meat platter by another slice, doused it with gravy and took it into her mouth in large chunks that left a smear of gravy in the space between her lower lip and her chin. Faro had a fleeting thought that it would be a lot of fun to lick her clean there, and wondered if some of her other appetites were as avid as that she displayed for food.

With an effort, he returned his attention to his landlady. "This's been mostly horse country, with mules for the freighting, and lately the railroads," he said. "Wouldn't of thought there'd be much call for bicycles, high-wheelers or this new kind."

Mrs. Pyle looked down the table, wincing a little as she caught sight of the nearly denuded meat platter, and said, "I don't understand the ins and outs of it, but when the major talks about his machines, why, you feel you got to have one or you won't be any way up to date. 'S promised me a lesson and a ride when he gets the ones that just come in all put together and in trim."

Faro wondered if the bicycle was made that would not buckle when mounted by Mrs. Pyle—unlike Holly O'Devie, she showed bountifully the effects of her good, solid cooking.

When the coffee and pie—a substantial share of it going to Holly O'Devie—were finished, Faro rose, rolled his napkin and stuck it into the china ring that had been set to the left of the fork at his place and excused himself. The train journey, with the broken sleep the lurching and rattling of the cars had allowed him, had caught up with him.

He made his way upstairs to the room he had been assigned, peeled off his jacket, took the flask of bourbon from his valise, ingested what he considered to be a reasonable sleeping dose and lay on the bed.

He awoke in midafternoon, feeling refreshed, but also untidy and sweaty under his clothes. Two days' accumulation of travel grime had sifted onto his skin, and he considered that it would be a good idea to get rid of it before he started on his rounds of Durgin.

Mrs. Pyle had told him that the boarders' bathroom was down the corridor. He went to it, tried the knob, found it unlocked and knocked. Hearing no answer, he opened the door and peered in, pleasantly surprised to see steam rising from the tin tub; he hadn't been sure that Mrs. Pyle had heard his tentatively expressed intention to treat himself to a bath about now, but evidently she had, and had seen to the supply of hot water. He began to unbutton his shirt, then caught sight of his face in the steamed mirror. Fuzzy around the chin and cheeks, no mistake. With the high cheekbones and pale green eyes and the bristly moustache, the two-day beard definitely gave him the appearance of a cougar, down from the mountains and aprowl for whatever prey he could find—not the kind of impression a man wants to give on his first night in a town where he hopes to persuade people that he's safe to gamble with. A shave was definitely in the cards. He returned to his room to get his gear and saw Holly

O'Devie stepping into a room diagonally across from his.

Faro had always been an impromptu packer rather than a methodical one, in spite of the fact that he was so often in transit and living out of his valise and tool case (which had on occasion harbored spare socks and other sundries as well as the necessities of his trade). Thus it took him some moments to come up with his shaving gear, which he recollected having rolled up in an extra pair of drawers. The first of these he uncovered revealed only his heavy artillery—the cut-down shotgun, shortened at both barrel and stock until it was little larger than an outdated dragoon pistol. He rarely used it in anger, as its display was usually enough to promote peaceableness and reason among men who moments before had felt otherwise. The second turned out to contain his cutthroat razor, a cake of soft soap for lather and a badger-hair brush.

Armed with these, he returned to the bathroom, also carrying the washbasin from the stand next to his bed, proposing to dip some hot water from the tub into the sink in the bathroom for shaving. He pushed the door open and stepped inside.

Black curls, black eyes, cream-pale face, red lips and a smooth column of throat rising from sloping shoulders rose from a froth of soapsuds in the tub.

"A good idea to knock first," Holly O'Devie said.

Chapter 3

"I, uh, I seed you going into your room just now," Faro said. "And as I'd checked at the bathroom just before, I figured it'd be empty."

"Well, it isn't, is it?" Holly O'Devie said. There was a froth of soapsuds across the steam-tendriled water, which went some way, but not very far, toward concealing her midsection. It clouded one breast completely, but the other just broke the surface, its pink tip flaccid and indrawn from the warmth and moisture. A steamy, soapy, flowery fragrance filled the room.

"I saw the tub full," Faro said huskily, "so I figure Ma Pyle had drawed it for me."

"No, it was for me," Holly O'Devie said, taking a washrag up and draping it over the exposed breast.

"Guess so," Faro said.

"Yes. And it really isn't big enough for two, Mr. . . ."

"Blake," Faro said, a little stung. He was not overly

30

prideful, but he was not used to having his name forgotten by a woman within a few hours of having been introduced to her. "Passed you the meat platter a couple times at lunch today."

"Oh, yes. Mr. Blake, do you always stand around making polite conversation when you've broken in on a lady having her bath? I am new to Arizona, but I haven't heard that that's a custom here."

"There is a story about that," Faro said, watching the pearly tints of her flesh waver under the water. "Fellow busts in like what I just did, accidental-like, and sees a woman in the bathtub. But he's a gentleman, see, and snaps his eyes shut and says, 'Excuse me, sir,' and backs out—see, he makes as if he'd thought it was another man, so's to spare the woman the shame of it."

"Mr. Blake, I don't care if you call me sir, colonel or Rutherford B. Hayes, but I wish you would get on out of here and leave me to wash without company," Holly O'Devie said.

A raft of soapsuds drifted slightly, revealing a dark patch below the pale rounded belly. "Uh," Faro said. "It's, uh, sometimes kind of hard to work the sponge around so's it gets to the middle of a person's back for a proper scrub. Easier for someone else to have the undertaking of that. So if—"

"Mr. Blake," Holly O'Devie said tartly, "if I find that I'm worrying myself into a decline over not being able to get six square inches or so of my back clean, I'll do my best imitation of a steam whistle and get Mrs. Pyle up here to help me. In fact, if you don't take yourself and your gear out of here right now, I am likely to do just that anyhow. If you want a bath and a shave, go down and arrange with her about that. But this bath's mine, and I don't propose to share it."

Half an hour later, shaved and letting the hot tub water soak away the grime and stiffness of travel, Faro reclined and stared at the tin-patterned ceiling. It seemed to him that the room was still redolent of the fragrance he had noticed when he had intruded on Holly O'Devie, and he could vividly imagine sharing the tub with her. And no saying that it mightn't come to that, or to something just as pleasant—she'd sent him on his way pretty sharply, no denying that, but on the other hand she hadn't been as upset or resentful as a lot of women would have been. The fact that she hadn't screamed the place down was a pretty good sign that, given the right circumstances, Holly O'Devie might not mind too much sharing a bathtub with him, or a bed or, come to that, a rug or a wall. A woman who could eat like that and not show it had to be burning up a lot of energy, one way or another, and it could be mighty pleasant to help her burn it up. . . .

The tip of his erection bobbed above the water, nudging the soapsuds aside. No time for that, he told himself sternly, and began scrubbing at his chest with the sponge. Best get your mind to business, Blake. Firstest thing, find a place to set up the bank, a place where Polk Pilchard's likely to turn up.

From its air of prosperity and prime location, across and a few doors down from the Butler House and not too near such haunts of respectability and female disapproval as the church and the milliner's, a neatly kept and carefully painted place called Callahan's was Faro's choice for a business address. He stepped into its cool shadowed interior out of the glare of the sun.

It was the dead hour of the afternoon, with the crowd that liked to drink their lunch long since departed and the evening patrons not yet arrived. There were only a couple of drinkers at the far end of the mahogany bar. Behind it stood a short plump man, dark-complexioned, with thinning black hair and a full drooping moustache. He was dressed in white cotton trousers and shirt and an ornate open vest heavily embroidered in silver. He was rearranging bottles on the shelves and humming a tune Faro recognized from his sojourn in Mexico back at the end of the War.

A Mexican bartender was something of a novelty, but not out of the way this far down, he supposed. "Uh . . . *por favor,*" he said to attract the man's attention.

The man turned. "Señor?"

"Uh, *quiero uno* . . ." Faro began, exhausting a good portion of his store of Spanish. *"Uno* . . . a glass of bourbon, *por favor."*

"Uno borbón, sí," the bartender said.

When the drink was brought, Faro paid for it and said, "The boss . . . *el jefe* . . . *es aquí?"*

The man grinned at him. "You min you wanning to see *el patrón,* ees that eet, señor?"

"Uh, *sí,"* Faro said. "I—"

He was interrupted by one of the men at the other end of the bar bawling, "Callahan!" and rapping his glass on the bar. To Faro's surprise, the bartender moved swiftly down the bar to the man and said, "Sure, ye'd wake the dead wid yer hollerin', Murphy. Ye'll not die of thirst for another second or so's waitin', and it'd do ye no harm to learn somethin' in the class of manners, so it wouldn't."

When the transaction was completed and the bartender returned, Faro looked at him thoughtfully. "Callahan?"

The bartender grinned. "Porfirio Callahan, at your service. Father Irish, mother Mexican. Me dad talked one way, Ma another and I picked up from both of 'em. Some of the customers is more comfortable with the

Mex side of me, others with the mick, so I give 'em what they fancy. It's the way of business, d'ye see?"

"Any of 'em fancy a little sporting diversion of an evening that they ain't getting?" Faro asked. "Faro and poker mainly, though I'll oblige in other directions, if called for. Oh, yeah—care to have a drink with me?"

"Thank you kindly, sir. Lemme see, tequila or the stuff that's something like stout that came in from St. Louis . . . believe I'll drink Irish-style for the moment, so the stout it is." Callahan poured the dark pungent brew into a glass, inspected the yellowish-brown head and gulped, then set the glass down and inspected Faro. "Had the idea that might be the way of it when I saw you," he said. "That rig's as much a sign as a bloody apron on a butcher. Well, sure, there's fellows that's interested in a flutter now and then, and there's nobody regular to take them on in a professional way. I'd not take kindly to any sharping, though—if there was any of that, likely you'd be out of town, either on a rail or in a box, but I'd still be here doing business, with a bad name onto the place."

"Not a good thing to have a bad name," Faro said equably, taking no offense at the saloonkeeper's implied question. "Happens I don't have one myself, for that sort of thing."

"But you do have a name?" Callahan said.

"Faro Blake."

"Ah. Heard of you, that I have, Mr. Blake. 'Tis said you're one of the few that runs a straight game of faro, and nothing known against you at poker. Well, well, welcome to Durgin, though I'll say it seems a small-potatoes kind of town for a man that's been used to the places and the players that you likely have." Callahan hoisted his glass in a saluting gesture and drank some more of its contents, which looked to Faro like something that might have been dredged out of the Mississippi.

"I hear there is at least one big potato around," Faro said. "Calls itself a Polk Pilchard."

"Ah," Callahan said. "Now, yes, Mr. Polk Pilchard has a fondness for poker, and he doesn't get the sort of play he likes at it hereabouts. Well, well, and would you be thinking you could provide him with such?"

"Might be," Faro said. "Figuring to study on it anyhow."

Callahan grinned. "And it's in your mind to start by finding out what you can about the man. No better place to start than the local saloon. Fair enough, though, now, I won't be gossiping about a customer, but I daresay you'll find someone here that wouldn't mind unloading a few opinions on Mr. Polk Pilchard over a drink or so, to the good of my trade." He shifted his gaze past Faro and said, *"Hola,* Señor Barnet."

Faro turned and nodded to the dry-goods merchant as he moved up to the bar and addressed Callahan in a rapid-fire stream of Spanish. Callahan replied in the same language—Faro caught the name Pilchard in the middle of it—then moved off to fetch Barnet a drink.

"How come the lingo?" Faro asked. "Wouldn't of picked you for a Mex, myself."

"I'm not—*gracias,* Porfirio," Barnet said as Callahan slid a glass of rye and water in front of him—"but a lot of my customers are, so I learned it, good for business, and I practice it with Callahan here when I can. He mentioned that you were starting to ask some about Polk Pilchard. Guess I caught your interest with what I was saying on the train last night, but I'd say he craves more in the way of big-time play than one man can give him."

"Maybe so," Faro said, "but it could be that I can

work out a way to accommodate him. Like Callahan was telling me just now, the thing in any line of work is to give the customer what he fancies."

Barnet waited a beat for further explanation of Faro's remark. When it was not forthcoming, he grunted and said, "Since I got back, I heard something that might make it a touch harder to get into Polk Pilchard for any important money, which I take it's your aim to do."

"What would that be?" Faro asked.

Barnet grinned. "I don't know the details, and it might be best for you to listen around and soak it up for yourself. Frankly, it sounds too damn foolish for me to pass on unless I'm dead sure of it."

At supper, with Mrs. Pyle once more lamenting the absence of Major Mordaunt—now reported to be instructing a mechanic in the assembly and tuning of his bicycles—Faro went over what he had learned. Not damn much. Barnet, still amused, had persisted in refusing to elaborate on his cryptic comment. From a couple of drinks with other patrons, Faro picked up that nobody would mind much if something happened to irritate, impoverish or injure Polk Pilchard, though no one was inclined to do anything about it himself. Also, Pilchard was married to a lady of outstanding good looks, of whose attributes he was widely rumored to be unable to make good use.

Scraps only, but likely, Faro considered, he would find out more during the course of the evening's play, as well as reencounter Pilchard, who drifted in most nights for a few—usually solitary—drinks. Anyhow, it seemed that, short of robbing Pilchard at gunpoint in broad daylight, he wouldn't have to worry about interference from the townsfolk of Durgin.

At Holly O'Devie's request, he passed over a slice of

ham from the platter next to him. Her third, I make it, Faro thought. My, she keeps on like that, won't be long before she won't fit in that tub. He studied the front of her dress, recalling the glimpse he had had of what was under it, and felt a stirring in his groin. It wasn't all that long since he had been with a woman, but there was something about Holly O'Devie, dressed or more or less concealed by soapsuds, that made it seem too long a time.

She looked up and caught the direction of his glance, perhaps divining the thought that went with it. In any case she reddened slightly and looked down at her plate. But there was a half-smile on her lips.

"Well, now," Polk Pilchard said, "looks as if my luck's running better back here than it did in Denver, just like I said."

"Seems so," Faro said. Pilchard had bet heavily and won a good many more turns than he had lost. He would have taken a substantial portion of Faro's resources if not for Faro's insistence on keeping to the standard limits. As it was, even with a few compensating losses from other players, he was definitely down for the evening. No matter, it meant that Pilchard was in a good mood and confident of his luck, which was just how Faro wanted him.

With the layout folded and placed in the case along with the casekeeper, dealing box and cards, Faro said, "Back in Denver, you was talking some mournful about not being able to travel and get into them big games you got such a shine to. Was thinking I could do something about that."

Pilchard shook his head. "No disrespect, Blake, but there's only one of you. What I crave is a whole bunch of fellows, ready to stake what they please, in tens, hundreds or thousands, and me with my luck running strong and going up against 'em. And that you can't provide."

Faro pulled two chairs over to the table on which he had run his bank and said, "Lemme get us a couple drinks and we could have a talk about just that."

Ten minutes later, Pilchard was fascinated but dubious. "You really think you could get them here— Gates, Lewis, the whole crowd?"

"Some of 'em, anyhow," Faro said. "See, I can wire Lewis that Gates and so on is going to sit in, and then wire Gates that Lewis and so on is, and the same with a bunch of the others. And once word gets around that even a few of 'em is coming, why, there'll be a rush to join in. And, way you tell me your luck runs whenas you're away from home, them that's run acrost you before'll figure you're going to go on losing and they might as well dip into the gravy."

Pilchard glanced at him shrewdly. "And maybe you've got some of the same sort of notion," he said. "What's in this for you, anyhow?"

"Enough," Faro said. "One, I get plenty of action with high-stakes players, which I normally ain't got the cash for. But, this setup, I can pick and choose when I want to sit in, 'stead of sticking through the whole thing. Two, you run it right and it'll get told of all around the country. Why, there'll be folks'll give me custom just to hear about it firsthand. Could be I'll win some off you, could be I'll lose to you, but there'll be plenty of others I can count on skimming a little from, all open and aboveboard. Plus which you're footing the bill for the whole thing, wires and all, one hell of a big spread and all the booze they can drink, so it ain't no expense out of my pocket."

"It'd be something," Pilchard said wistfully. "They'd be talking about it for years, Polk Pilchard's big game, just like they do about some of McGaha's and Osborne's. And it'd about knock the eyes out of some of the folks here in Durgin, just wouldn't it!"

"And with that luck of yours, you'd likely walk away the big winner," Faro said with false heartiness. "Taking it for granted, of course, that you got the cash to back you on your play."

"Oh, yes, I've . . . " Pilchard said, looking all the same a touch uneasy. "But there's . . . Well, look, I've got to think on it. I don't deny I'm powerfully taken with the idea, but . . . Listen, you come and see me tomorrow, have lunch with me and we'll talk it over some more, huh? At the west end of Front Street, you can't miss it, only two-story stone house in Durgin."

After Pilchard's departure, Faro pondered briefly on what was causing his hesitation—probably tied in with Barnet's hint that afternoon, but that didn't go further toward explaining it—then rose from the table and headed for the bar for a last bourbon or so before returning to Mrs. Pyle's.

He stopped as he heard a familiar voice raised in conversation with Callahan. ". . . a turn of speed you wouldn't believe, my dear fellow, and nearly effortless except for the healthful and beneficial exercise involved," a tall man leaning on the bar was saying. He was facing away from Faro, but the shock of white hair in the style of the late President Jackson and the long, claw-hammer coat were as sure identification as a full-face photograph.

"The sporting elements are only secondary," the man went on. "Commerce, a reliable mode of travel— and consider the military applications! An infantry detachment delivered silently and in stealth to wherever is required, and no clattering, neighing horses or creaking of wagon wheels to betray them—the age of lightning warfare will have arrived. And it's not beyond American ingenuity to contrive a light engine of some sort to fit onto them, for tireless and perpetual travel. I know for a fact that Edison is working on something along those lines right now."

Faro grinned and moved to the bar next to the speaker, who started and looked at him sharply as he ordered a bourbon from Callahan.

Faro raised his glass and nodded. "We ain't yet met," he said, "but I b'lieve we're fellow boarders at Ma Pyle's. Name of Blake, in the gambling line. And I'd put a pretty good stake on it that you're Major Mordaunt, the bicycle magnate."

"You have the right of it, sir. Major Hilary Mordaunt, late of the Queen's Own Rifles, now proud to be traveling for Macduff and Sons of Springfield, Massachusetts, manufacturers of the most advanced models yet known. Honored to meet you, Mr. Blake," Doc Prentiss said.

Chapter 4

"I always admire to hear about new machines and things, Major," Faro said. "How about I fetch us a bottle and you and me retire to a table whereas we can discuss how everybody's going to wheel into the twentieth century?"

"Glad to have a new ear for my passion," Doc said. "I fear our good host, to say nothing of the rest of the honest Durgin townsfolk, have begun to tire of my enthusiasm for the excellent devices I have the privilege to represent. Lead on, Mr. Blake."

With bottle and two glasses in hand, Faro preceded Doc to a table in the corner, well away from any hearers. He reflected that what he had just said to Doc was a flat and substantial lie. In his experience, modern inventions usually meant trouble. That business over in Texas with the talking machines had landed him and Doc in jail, and nearly got them drowned, shot and

41

shelled by a warship. And the stint with the traveling photographer had thrown him in with that maniac gunman, Turkey Nickerson, who had alternated between trying to recruit him for his gang and trying to kill him. Once the scientists and engineers had come up with the really good stuff, like the great old Mississippi side-wheelers, the Pullman car and the magnetically controlled roulette wheel, Faro felt, it was time to stop. Doc Prentiss in combination with some new kind of machinery struck him as having explosive potential, no matter if it was something as harmless as a bicycle. Doc would find a way to land himself and anybody in with him on the scam in deep shit—but at least this time Faro wasn't involved.

"Well, now, Doc," he said when they were seated, in a low voice calculated not to carry far, "what is all this about? What I hear at the boardinghouse, you got these bicycles in and are drumming up custom for them, and that's about it. Are you for God's sake setting up in an honest line of work?"

"Your cynicism pains me, young Faro," Doc said, sipping at his whiskey. "That remark about honest work is a slur unworthy of you. I am a confidence man, not a damned drummer. I admit that the bicycles I have on consignment from Macduff are quite as excellent as I claim, and will be delivered in working order, and are even worth close to half of what I will charge for them. But you know me well enough to be sure that that is only part of the trappings of the game."

"I don't see what kind of games you can play with a couple wheels and eight pounds or so of iron tubing," Faro said.

"Quite a few," Doc said. "One of them based on the facts that like horses, one will go faster than another, and that people think that that's worth bothering about—and betting on."

Recalling Gates and his pals and the two raindrops, Faro had to agree. "Don't see how you could fix bicycle races, though," he said. "I mean, you can't dope the horse or bribe the jockey, as I expect it'd be the owners theirselfs in the saddle, and set on winning for the pride of it."

"There are at least six ways to bring about any desired result in such a contest," Doc said, "and I am up on the details of all of them. However, I don't expect to use the knowledge except in self-defense, as, if the race I want to promote takes place, I'll be in charge of it, and it would raise eyebrows more than considerably if I were to act as bookmaker as well. The thing about this is not who wins, but what he wins."

"What is that going to be?"

"A massive cup of pure gold, cleverly engraved with scenes of cyclists enjoying themselves in a variety of ways—the First Annual Durgin Cycle Trophy. That's for the overall winner. There will be smaller but proportionately valuable mementos for the winners of separate events such as the half-mile heat, distance, endurance and speed at repairing a damaged wheel."

"Hey, now," Faro said, "I don't somehow see a New Englander named Macduff being sudden took all that generous, just to help sell off a few bicycles."

"Of course not," Doc said. "The notion is to arouse an interest amounting to fever in the contest, and lavish awards are a sure way to do that. I have interested a local man of substance in the proposition, and he is studying it carefully. It would put Durgin on the map, which would benefit him through his many investments, and would give him no end of personal satisfaction. It is a trivial detail that, once the gold is available, it will be up to the one expert around on cycling matters to convey it to the craftsman who will fashion the trophies and return with them."

"Which you ain't about to do," Faro said.

Doc shook his head. "That would be unprofessional, mere theft, and the kind of thing precautions would be taken against. No, I shall return with the trophies and cheerfully submit them to any tests for genuineness. In fact, I shall return with two sets of trophies, one made up at my own expense, of the finest amalgam of brass and lead, expensively plated in genuine gold, and undistinguishable from the real article by weight or feel. Unless scratched with a penknife by some soul harboring unworthy suspicions, they will give years of harmless and prideful pleasure when displayed on the whatnot cabinet."

"Slick, if it works," Faro said.

"It will work," Doc assured him. "And that's not the whole of it, by any means." He refilled his glass, drank from it and looked fondly at Faro. "But enough of my affairs for the moment, young Faro. What brings you to this unlikely burg? Done something to make your usual haunts too hot for you?"

Faro explained his plans for establishing Polk Pilchard as a legendary gambler and host. Doc looked at him intently as he concluded, "So I ought to be able to pick up a couple thousand or so, maybe a hell of a lot more, sitting in on some of them games, along with getting me a name that'll do me good in business. Don't expect this Pilchard will get much out of it in the end, but that's his lookout."

"An interesting scheme, my dear boy," Doc said mildly. "It shows an ability to plan which I own I had not seen in you before. A pity that it won't work."

"Why won't it?" Faro asked.

"Because Pilchard's my pigeon—or fish, I suppose, would be a more accurate image. I have him just about on the hook, and I don't propose to have him wriggle off, just to get involved in your enterprise."

"Hell, Doc," Faro protested, surprised at the steely note in the old man's voice, "whatever them trophies come to, it can't amount to more'n a few thousand, and Pilchard's got enough not to miss it more'n you would a half-dollar that'd dropped through a hole in your pocket."

"Sure," Doc said. "And what makes you think I'd go to all this trouble for that kind of score? It's worth picking up, of course, and I don't intend to overlook it. But the big thing is to get this Pilchard convinced that bicycles are the rage, that the deserts will be covered with legions of cyclists, that for most purposes they will replace the horse—in short, that there is one hell of a lot of money to be made by a substantial and early investment. When his ears are ringing with the plaudits of the crowd as he presents the awards to the winners, he can't help but feeling that he's in on the beginning of something big. And it is just about then that he will discover an opportunity to invest in the manufacturer of these nonpareil machines, Macduff of Springfield. More than just invest, acquire a number of shares sufficient to afford him control of the company, with the connivance of Major Hilary Mordaunt, whose chief ambition is to become vice-president and sales manager."

"Don't seem like a job you'd care for, Doc," Faro said.

"Well, naturally not—I'd sooner be dead in a ditch. But that's the last little barb on the hook, a nice venal motive for me that doesn't compete with Pilchard's interests, and of course makes the necessity for clandestine dealings plain. So he'll understand why there won't be any dealings with brokers, just Major Mordaunt using sources he knows to collect and deliver the needed shares to their new proprietor, in return for a small commission—if I were to do it free and gratis, he'd get suspicious—and the promise of the job Major Mordaunt covets."

"I got a idea of what them sources is," Faro said.

Doc nodded. "An excellent printer and engraver in Phoenix, can do you up a stock certificate that looks as official and rich as a greenback. Rumor has it that he's tried his hand at those, too, back East, but they never could make anything stick in court."

"What happens when Pilchard writes off to Springfield and announces he has took over and Major Mordaunt is now in charge of selling the stuff?" Faro asked.

Doc grinned. "If I time it right, the letter'll come back or go to the dead-letter office. Macduff's is about to go into bankruptcy, and by the time the stock's delivered, likely they will have, and there'll be nobody there to open the mail. They put too much capital into this new line of cycles and haven't been able to sell enough of 'em—that's why they were willing to let me have this batch on consignment, with nothing down. They'll go bust within a month, I know that from nosing around there on one of my rare visits to the Atlantic shores. Now, if they'd actually had Major Mordaunt managing sales, it'd have been a different story. The major, or Colonel Humphrey Rowayton or Chief Spotted Tail," Doc said, naming two of his frequently employed aliases, "to say nothing of Jackson Lafitte Prentiss, could have bedridden grandmothers and peglegged sailors lining up to buy the machines. It's a great loss to the nation's economy that I never turned my talents to the ordinary varieties of commerce, I must say."

"Well, you're good at what you do, for sure, Doc," Faro said. "But what's that got to do with—"

"Damn it, young Faro, don't you see? I intend to take this Pilchard for a big chunk of what he has. I mean, a man that wants to take over a thriving firm like Macduff has to expect to pay out heavily for the chance. And it's one thing to do that when there's no other major calls on your resources, and no other way to get a big name and make some money, and another when there's competition for your funds and an alternate way of getting the kind of satisfaction you crave. You and I are working the same side of the street, boy, and there isn't room enough for both of us on the plankwalk."

"And you are figuring it's for me to step off of it," Faro said slowly.

"That's it," Doc said. "I was on the spot first, and, as you'll admit, what I'm after is a good deal more substantial than the benefits possibly accruing from your scheme, however well thought out. Because of our long-standing relationship, I have no objection, of course, to a reasonable compensation for pulling out, payable after the scam is complete and the proceeds are in hand."

"Hey, Doc," Faro said, "less leave the substantials out of it and forget about the compensations. I seed this fish out in Denver, a good while back, and I been studying on how to work on him since, and I don't propose to back off on him. I won't queer your pitch, but if it comes to who steps off of the plankwalk, I am telling you it won't be Faro Blake."

Doc looked at him closely. "You'll recall those old days on the river, when you were a mere lad, and your father, my old friend A. B., had me instruct you in the rudiments of culture and literature, providing you with the only education you ever had?" Aaron Burr Blake had indeed arranged with his friend and contemporary Prentiss to tutor his half-orphaned son as the confidence man and the gambler conducted their trade on the luxurious riverboats that plied the Mississippi in the decade before the War. All the same . . . .

"I recall 'em, Doc," Faro said. "And recalling don't cut no ice. A grown-up and a kid, that's one thing, but when there's two grown-ups into it, why, then they're toe to toe. You being older than me and knowing me when I was a tad don't apply. We been through some things since them days, and each of us played our parts as men, and helped each other—and sometimes me a lot more than you, if you'll call a couple things to mind—but I figure to do what I come here to do, and I ain't going to back off from it."

Faro sucked the last drop from his flask of bourbon and set it down beside the bed. He stared up into the darkness, wishing for sleep—it had to be past four by now, he thought—but unable to drift off, bone-tired though he was. He found himself going over the argument with Doc, wondering what he could have said to make it come out differently. After they had left Callahan's, they had walked back together to Mrs. Pyle's, advancing their claims to Pilchard's funds with increasing heat, each digging ever harder into his own position and preparing to bring artillery to bear on the other.

"Damn it, boy," Doc had said, "you're being a dog in the manger. You're just going after what you could get in a hundred places out of a hundred men—but for me Pilchard's a rare chance, a rich man that can be taken for a hell of a lot of what he's got. You pull out of here tomorrow and you'll hardly notice the difference."

"Well, I ain't, Doc," Faro had said. "You got a lot of years on me, and we go back a long ways, but I don't step aside for no man. You knowed A. B., and you know me, so you know you can't figure on a Blake crawfishing."

"Nor on a Mordaunt," Doc said. "I have a name to uphold, even if it's only a borrowed one."

By the time they parted at the bottom of the front staircase at Mrs. Pyle's, with Doc headed for his first-floor room, Faro for his quarters upstairs, they had not quite come to shouting or blows, but that was about the best thing that could be said. Doc had one last comment. "Remember, young Faro, I taught you a hell of a lot when you were a kid. But not everything. You think you can take me on this, you may have a surprise or so coming."

Now Faro stared upward, seeing nothing but the dark. No shit about it, he thought, Doc and me is on the same track and aimed to collide with all steam up. Don't feel right to go up against the old bugger, but there it is. Come morning, I'll study out what to do about him.

He was aware with relief that at last there was only a tiny bubble of consciousness remaining to him, and that it was dwindling fast. Just before sleep claimed him, he had the uneasy thought that Doc had had several decades' more experience at dealing with unwanted obstacles than he himself had. No denying it, Doc could have some pretty nasty tricks up his sleeve, and seemed as if he was prepared to use them. . . .

Faro came awake, facedown in the pillow, with a convulsive twitch. He turned over and looked out the window. By the sun, it was mid- to late morning, not much more than an hour or so before he was due at Polk Pilchard's house for lunch and a talk about setting up the big game. He ran his fingers over his chin; yes, there was enough rasp on his fingertips so that he'd better shave before then. No need for a bath though; he hadn't been running or doing anything to work up a sweat, so that yesterday's would hold him well enough.

In his shirt sleeves and socks, carrying the basin from his night stand, he padded downstairs to the kitchen and had the basin filled with hot water. "My washing day," Mrs. Pyle said, "and I don't know how I'm to get it done, all you people wanting hot water at all hours. Well, never mind, I can heat some more up fast enough, I s'pose."

Back in his room, Faro soaped and shaved, wondering how to handle the business of fighting Doc for Pilchard. Stubborn old bastard should have the sense just to cut out of it, he thought. But I don't expect he will.

Lightheaded from the lack of sleep, he contemplated the soapy water in the basin, flecked with the debris of his beard, with disfavor. Nothing to have lying around the room, for sure; best empty it out in the bathroom sink.

He took the basin and walked down the hall, then pushed open the bathroom door. "Oh, Jesus. Sorry, ma'am." Did Holly O'Devie live in the damn tub?

"Mr. Blake." Her voice had an undercurrent of amusement as she slid down beneath the froth of soapsuds, leaving only her black-ringleted head exposed. "I hear—That is, you seem to make a habit of this."

"No more'n you make a habit of having a bath," Faro said. "Expect you're about the cleanest young lady in Durgin, or maybe in all the Territory."

"Arizona's a lot dustier than California," Holly O'Devie said.

"I just come in to empty out thisyer basin," Faro said. The odd lightheadedness he had become aware of in his room was still with him, and made the fact that he was conversing with a naked fellow boarder in the bathtub seem reasonably normal, especially as Holly O'Devie didn't seem to be raising any objections to it. I do this often enough, he thought, and I expect we'll both of us get used to it.

"Good," Holly O'Devie said. "If you wanted a bath, there wouldn't be room. Though I'm about finished, and I wasn't all that dirty, so you could use the water after me. It's still hot."

The air in the room was steamy and held a strong scent, as it had yesterday, though it seemed to Faro that it was a different fragrance. He wondered if Holly O'Devie had a different bath soap for every day in the week. He also wondered why Holly O'Devie wasn't ordering him out of the bathroom immediately, as she had yesterday. The funny way he was feeling, there was no harm in finding out.

He emptied the basin into the sink and wiped it with the tail of his shirt. "If you're finished washing up, I'd admire to help you dry off," he said. "My experience, a person does that hisself, he leaves wet places and his clothes stick to them."

"I hate sticky clothes," Holly O'Devie said dreamily. "The towel's hanging from a hook on the door."

She grasped the edges of the tub and levered herself upward, then stood. Water and suds rippled from her, one evanescent raft of them foundering in the black crispness between her thighs. She raised one dripping thigh high and stepped from the tub onto the bathmat. He took the towel from the door and stepped toward Holly O'Devie, who looked at him calmly. Her face was very close to his as he bunched the rough cloth and rubbed it over her shoulders, down her breasts and belly and legs; then she turned and he completed drying her. Along with the lightheadedness, he felt pulses pounding in his head and throat, and a stiffness and swelling in his groin.

"You dry now?" he asked.

She picked her wrapper from the floor and put it around her. "Not everywhere," she said.

"Where— Oh."

Holly O'Devie nodded. "Toweling's not what's called for for that," she said. "Take a look outside and see if there's anybody in the hall. Wouldn't do for someone to see a man and a woman coming out of the bathroom at the same time. They'd think we were up to something scandalous."

"I expect we is, or will be, ain't we?" Faro said, still feeling giddy and half-convinced he was on an unusual run of luck.

"I certainly hope so," Holly O'Devie said.

A minute later, having successfully navigated the hallway without being observed, they were in Faro's room. Holly O'Devie's wrapper whispered to the floor; Faro's urgent fingers detached a shirt button from its moorings as he wrenched his garments away.

It was only when his erection slid into Holly O'Devie's slick, enfolding warmth and her thighs clamped around him, and her breasts shook as she moved in response to his thrust, that he was fully sure he was awake—or else had found a way of dreaming that he would as soon keep on with for one hell of a long time.

The light smell of perfumed soap that rose from her cool flesh mingled with her sharper personal scent from where he moved in and out of her. Her hands slid over his chest and back and thighs, stroking, then digging with the edges of her fingernails. He cupped one breast with his hand and rubbed his thumb across the dark nipple, feeling it harden and seeing it swell. She brought her hand up to his, squeezing her breast until the nipple rose toward his mouth. He bent, tasted it, then gently took it between his teeth; she gave a sound something between a mew and a purr, and pressed his head against her.

Faro reached down and slid his hand between her buttocks and the bed sheet, raising her a trifle, and probed between her thighs, behind where his damp erection pistoned. His forefinger sought and found, penetrated, moving to the rhythm of his thrusts. Holly O'Devie arched and gasped beneath him.

When he felt the power of the explosive contractions within her, he let himself come to his own climax, and they subsided, gasping for breath and shuddering in the aftermath of their ecstasy.

After quite a while, Faro raised himself up on one elbow and looked at Holly O'Devie, who was gazing unfocusedly at the ceiling. "I ain't complaining a bit, no, sir," he said, "but that is quite some way of getting acquainted. Yestiddy when I bust in on you in the tub, you was some standoffish, as is what you might expect to happen in the run of things, but, same thing today and it works out different. You mind telling me how come?"

"Oh," Holly O'Devie said, "it's just that I didn't know you well enough then. But you're so polite about passing the food at dinner and supper, I guess I just took a shine to you."

What would of happened, Faro wondered, if I had of give her a whole ham?

Chapter 5

The recollection of Holly O'Devie's yielding body was fresh in Faro's mind, and something of her scent still clung about him, but he had little difficulty in imagining what Mrs. Polk Pilchard would look like, peeled of the rose-pink velvet gown she was wearing. She was a good bit taller than Holly, and lush in proportion, with smooth blond hair rather than dark curls. Faro imagined himself undoing the front of the gown and letting the full breasts pop free; they seemed to be wanting to do that on their own, as it was, every time she bent over her plate.

Can see why the men in town think Pilchard's a fool for spending his evenings at Callahan's, Faro thought. A woman like that in the house, I'd be putting my time in at home. Big place like this, there's lots of places to have fun. He imagined pleasuring himself with Mrs. Pilchard on the parlor rug, which had felt as thick and soft as some mattresses he had slept on, or on the overstuffed sofa there, or on the green-felt billiard table Pilchard had proudly displayed, or on the dining room table—maybe fully set, with Mrs. P.'s frantically scissoring legs kicking crystal and silver every which way. . . . And Pilchard had told of, but not shown, four bedrooms upstairs, and a bathroom with oversized tub and running hot and cold water—the tub sounded big enough for two, easy.

This train of thought was made almost inevitable by the fact that Polk Pilchard's house was decorated and furnished with a gaudy opulence like a high-class brothel, running to a lot of velvet upholstery, gilt and crystal chandeliers, textured wallpaper, knicknacks in every corner, shawls draped on the piano and cushions strewn about anyplace there was room for them. Faro supposed that a good whorehouse was the nearest to luxurious living that Pilchard had encountered in his prospecting days, so it made sense for him to have re-created one for himself when he struck it rich. Certainly Mrs. Pilchard could have fit into the best of them, and no questions asked.

He wrenched his mind back to what he had been saying and took a mouthful of the roast lamb on his plate to give himself time to recollect exactly what it was.

"Oh, yeah," he said, when the meat had been chewed and swallowed. "Anyhow, this fellow, he got the others in the game to agree to it, and he took his hand and left the place, two of the others going with him to see to fair play. And he went acrost the street to the bank and ast to see the top man. So they loosed him onto the head clerk, and he says, 'I want to take out a loan for five thousand.' And the clerk says, 'What security?' And the fellow shows him the hand, four kings, remember? and he says, 'I'm in a game at the place acrost the street, and here's my hand, four kings.

There's been a ace up in the hand of a man that folded, so there's no way these can be beat, but I got to have the cash to see and raise, as they won't take my marker'—thass like a note of hand, ma'am," Faro said, noting a look of inquiry on Mrs. Pilchard's face.

" 'So,' this fellow says, 'thass my security for the loan.' Well, the clerk, he says, 'My good man, you got to be crazy. Thass no security for a loan, a hand of cards.' And he walked the fellow away and out of the bank, and them that was with him. And as they was going out of the bank, up comes the president of it and asks what's going on. And the clerk, he tells him, and the president, he says, 'Give the man the money he wants. And you better remember,' he says, 'that four kings in a game like that is good for any kind of loan in this bank—right up to the last cent we got.' The president being a poker-playing man, see, so knowing what it meant."

Polk Pilchard gave a sigh of mingled pleasure and wistfulness, and said, "That's the style, that's the way to do things, for fair. Not the Durgin way, though, no real spirit in the men here."

"A very interesting story, Mr. Blake," Mrs. Pilchard said in her deep throaty voice. "Did the man win the money and pay back the loan?"

"Well, he had to, 'Melia," Pilchard said testily. "With one ace accounted for, wasn't a hand possible that could beat him."

"Well, I don't know that much about cards, Mr. Pilchard, as you well know," she said. "I do my solitaire and that's it."

"Kid's game," Pilchard said.

"Well, I like it. It's sort of fun, making up stories as the hand plays out, the queen goes down on the king, and then the jack goes down on the queen, and so on."

Faro, taking a sip at his glass of wine, sputtered and

gave a sharp glance at Mrs. Pilchard, who smiled at him blandly. It was wonderful how ladies that didn't know much of the low side of life could fall into saying what sounded like some pretty strong stuff by accident, he thought.

"Well, you take it, 'Melia," Pilchard said, "four kings with an ace out, that's a hand that'll take the pot, for sure."

"Is that so, Mr. Blake?" Mrs. Pilchard asked.

"Seed it come out another way once," Faro said. Pilchard gave him a startled look. "Over in Ellsworth, in Kansas, a few years back, was in a game in the Blue Dog Saloon. There wasn't no ace showing, but a fellow laid down four kings and he reached for the pot. And another fellow says, 'Not so fast, there, I think this beats that,' and he lays down his hand."

"Four aces?" Pilchard said.

"Nope. Royal flush."

"But—oh."

"Yeah," Faro said.

"Which of them won?" Mrs. Pilchard asked.

"Neither one," Faro said. "The man with the flush had his shooter out sooner'n you can say 'knife,' and plugged the man with the kings, but the man with the kings had a pocket gun under the table and got off a shot that done for the other man before he cashed in."

"I don't understand," Mrs. Pilchard said.

"For— Listen, 'Melia, there's only four kings in a deck of cards, d'you see? And a royal flush has got to have a king into it, so with four kings and a royal flush, there's a fifth king been rung into the game by someone."

"I see," Mrs. Pilchard said. She looked toward Faro. "Which one of them did it?"

"Nobody never knowed," Faro said, "them closest concerned being in no condition to give information."

The hired girl who had served the lunch entered the dining room and said, "Man at the door to see you, Mr. Pilchard."

Pilchard gave Faro a glance that seemed almost furtive, and said, "Matter of business, excuse me a minute, Blake." He rose and left the room.

"You must lead an interesting life, Mr. Blake," Amelia Pilchard said. She took a long gulp of the red wine in the glass at her place, and then another, setting it down almost empty, and gave Faro a glittering smile. "Going where you please, doing what you want to do."

"I ain't one for sticking in one place a long time," Faro said.

"There's something fascinating about that to someone like me, who's stuck in one place," Amelia Pilchard said. "I don't think I'd like being on the move constantly myself, but I'm intrigued to meet someone who's here today and gone tomorrow, so to speak. It's sort of stifling to know only people you've known for years and years and will be knowing for years and years—they remember everything, so you have to be so careful with them, what you say and what you do. Someone like you, I could . . . oh, I don't know, but, whatever it was, it wouldn't be around to be fetched up to me once you were gone."

"There is that," Faro said vaguely. While he was wondering if Mrs. Pilchard could possibly have meant what she seemed to be meaning, Polk Pilchard returned to the dining room and resumed his seat.

After the hired girl had taken away the plates and in a few moments brought in coffee and some watery ice cream, Mrs. Pilchard said, "Do you run across many cheats in your work, Mr. Blake?"

"There are some," Faro said, "but most of the shady fellows I see as I'm going about is in the confidence-game line, in some way. There was Canada Bill, for instance, that used to pass himself off as a reverend. He would travel the trains and get passengers into a little card cutting to pass the time. Him being a minister, the fellows he tried it on didn't see no harm, and, what with one thing and another, it'd pretty soon work out that Bill had about all the other fellow's cash and maybe his watch and return ticket, and was about in tears at what the Lord's bounty would mean to his flock. So the fellow that got took, he hardly had the sand to raise a ruckus about it. So that's sharping and conning all into one."

"You hear a lot about the confidence game, the green-goods merchants, the goldbrick salesmen and so on," Pilchard said. "I don't know how they get away with it, the men that get taken must have an attic to let and no tenants applying. I'd like to see one of that crowd try anything on Polk Pilchard—I'd send him packing so fast, the dust wouldn't settle for a week."

"Some of them is pretty clever," Faro said, finding it hard to keep from either gritting his teeth in rage or bursting into laughter. "There is this fellow Doc Prentiss that I've heard of, that is said to be slick as a slippery elm."

"Well, you see this Prentiss sometime, you can tell him it's no use his bothering with Polk Pilchard. I didn't get where I am by not being able to see into a millstone better than most."

I could hull Doc below the waterline and sink him with all hands, Faro thought, just by dropping the word right now. So why the hell don't I?

When the hired girl cleared the table, Pilchard said, "Let's you and me get on into the study, Blake, and go over that matter we was discussing last night."

Faro bowed as Amelia Pilchard left the room, then followed Pilchard down a hallway and into an oak-paneled room lined with bookshelves. The backs of the books displayed seemed to have been carved out of long pieces of wood and painted to resemble the real thing; a moth-eaten moose head glowered at them from one wall.

"Man has to have a place of his own to do his thinking," Pilchard said, gesturing pridefully. "I don't expect even J. P. Morgan has got a room fitted out like this one."

"Nor he doesn't, I'd say," Faro said.

For a quarter of an hour the two men sipped at brandy that Pilchard poured from a cut-glass decanter, while Faro pitched the advantages of extending hospitality to the high-stakes players whose company he craved. "Even in Frisco and New York, they'll be talking it up," Faro said. "Sure, it'll cost a heap, but it'll be worth it. And if you mean what you said about your luck, you'll come out way ahead, anyhow. All the fellows that hang out at Callahan's, they'll be crowding the street outside your house and looking through the windows to see what's going on, and telling each other what a real sport Polk Pilchard is."

Pilchard was clearly entranced by the prospect, but clearly also unwilling to commit himself to it. "There is other considerations," he said finally, "and I guess I will have to think on it some more. Give you an answer in a day or so, Blake, so I will."

It was clear to Faro that Polk Pilchard was suffering deep spiritual agony over the question of whether his poker game or Doc's cycle race would give him more value, in the way of public appreciation and personal self-esteem, for his money.

When Pilchard led him to the front door, Faro spied a new element in the clutter of the entrance hall. A shiny bicycle, its paintwork gleaming, stood propped against one wall.

That'd be the "matter of business" this Pilchard took off to see to, Faro thought bitterly, taking delivery of one of Doc's damn cycles. Shit, I should of blowed the whistle on him at lunch. And I still could.

And I know damned well I won't. Someday I'd best work out why.

Chapter 6

It was chicken night at Mrs. Pyle's, and Faro's fork clashed with those of the other boarders as they went for the steaming slices of white meat laid out on platters. He noticed that Holly O'Devie avoided the competition for the preferred meat and concentrated on loading her plate with drumsticks, three for the first helping. One of these she was now chewing on industriously, the crisp skin crackling between her even white teeth and the rich juices running down her chin.

Way she's eating, Faro thought, she might of missed lunch. But I kind of doubt it. He caught her eye and gave her a quick smile—after all, it wasn't above eight hours since they had been giving each other the kind of good time that it warms a man and a woman to think about.

She returned his look coolly, betraying no recollection of that morning's encounter and its aftermath in his room, then returned her attention to the drumstick.

There was little of it but bones now, and she switched to the next one with the same avidity.

Faro was a little stung by her seeming indifference to him. Not that he'd have expected her to announce to the whole assembly what they'd been at earlier in the day, nothing like that, but when two people have humped each other silly a short while ago, it figured that there would be a little recognition of that the next time they met. But as far as he could see, the main—the only—thing on Holly O'Devie's mind was the chicken leg she was gnawing.

I want to get next to her another time, Faro thought; maybe I better arrange with Ma Pyle for a bucket of drumsticks and gravy, and fetch them along to her room late in the nighttime. Way to a man's heart is through his stomach, they say, and it looks like it works that way with a woman's twitchet—this one's, anyway. With quick clarity, a picture came to his mind of Holly O'Devie writhing under him, one hand running over him while the other held a drumstick to her mouth, its juices lubricating their bodies as they thrust in unison.

Once again, as at the other meals Faro had taken at Mrs. Pyle's, a vacant chair announced the absence of both Major Hilary Mordaunt and Jackson Lafitte Prentiss. Faro was relieved that Doc was not there—they had parted on bad terms, and it would take some hard thinking to work out what to do about that. Something Faro didn't understand clearly kept him from queering Doc's pitch, as he could easily have done. It wouldn't even be necessary to prove that Major Mordaunt was the notorious Doc Prentiss—the suggestion alone would arouse enough suspicion so that Doc's scheme would fail. But somehow it just didn't seem to be in the cards.

Holly O'Devie took a fourth drumstick. When Faro looked across the table again, it had gone. Quick eating, for sure, he thought. But there were only three bones on her plate. Wrapped in a handkerchief, he supposed, in case she got taken with a fit of the hungries in the night.

"Major Mordaunt told me you had a nice talk last night, when you and him met at Callahan's, Mr. Blake," Mrs. Pyle said. "Said you had a good discussion about your lines of work, but that he'd bet his would come out better than yours in the long run, as you've got to gamble, but he's working on a sure thing."

"He knows his line, I know mine," Faro said. "Expect we'll each do well enough to satisfy ourselves." He took his watch from his vest pocket and consulted it. "But if I'm to make my living at it, I'd best be on my way soon, ma'am."

"Just about like that story you told me this afternoon, Blake," Polk Pilchard said. "Only one less king."

Faro looked sourly at the royal flush Pilchard had laid down and at his own three kings. Holding the ten through the ace, less the jack, only an idiot would have been asked to be hit for one card—taking three would have given him a chance at a pair of aces, queens or kings, at least a playable hand. But one it had been for Pilchard, and that one the jack. He had figured Pilchard to be bluffing on the final composition of his hand, and had seen and reraised him with confidence, which he now saw to have been severely misplaced.

"Now, that is something to have brought off, Pilchard," Barnet said. The only other man in the game, conducted at a table against the rear wall of Callahan's, he had folded after the first round of betting. "Why, yes, sir, that is some poker playing to have seen. I would have bet that Blake would have taken the pot easy. And I surely would have been wrong, wouldn't I? Well, well."

Pilchard bloomed visibly under Barnet's appreciative comment. "Well, I guess I can play poker as well's I do other things," he said. "Matter of knowing the cards and knowing your luck, all there is to it. And then knowing how to play what you get. Blake, here, was sure I was bluffing when I raised, and so I was, sort of—bluffed him into thinking I was bluffing, d'you see, when I had a hand nothing could beat. That's how you come out ahead when you're playing with the real top kind of people, Barnet, know the cards and know your man."

I could snake out the Reid's from my vest under the table and put six slugs in this jasper's gut, quick as winking, Faro thought wistfully. Then he wouldn't be bragging so big about knowing his man. But folks would talk, and I don't expect I'd draw much custom after, let alone being maybe hanged for it. "I got to admit you foxed me there," he said with forced heartiness. "Expect, was you in a game with some of the really big poker men, you could sweep a damn good share of the pots, way you play."

"I don't doubt it," Pilchard said, "and it might be that it could come to that."

Faro's sour mood lightened, even though Pilchard was now raking in the pot. Lost money wasn't all lost, if it put Pilchard in the frame of mind to look favorably on Faro's proposition, especially now that he had had a little taste of the approbation and inflated reputation that he seemed to want.

This optimistic thought lasted only until Pilchard's departure, which he watched from Callahan's front door. The ex-mineowner left the saloon and went to a hitching post in front of it against which leaned the bicycle Faro had seen in his hallway that afternoon.

Pilchard mounted it with some difficulty, but managed to get it into a wavering forward momentum just sufficient to keep him from being pitched into the street, and moved down toward his house. His progress was accompanied by encouraging cries from the small crowd that had gathered to watch the unusual spectacle: "Go it, Polk!" "Whose buggy you steal them wheels off of, Polk?"

As Faro saw it, curiosity had drawn the crowd and derision occasioned their comments. But he suspected that the fact that there was a crowd, and that they were calling his name, however mockingly, would be enough for Polk Pilchard.

One step ahead, one back, was how it seemed to him.

Laden with oatmeal, fried eggs, frizzled ham, toast and coffee—Mrs. Pyle made sure that her boarders didn't go unfed, never mind if a boarder's idea of breakfast was an egg beaten up in brandy, with the egg optional—Faro walked down Front Street toward the shed where Major Mordaunt had set up his enterprise.

Wouldn't do no good to pull a gun on him and tell him to get out of town, Faro thought gloomily. He'd know damned well I wouldn't use it. And I don't see it's worth a pint of spit trying to get him to lay off Pilchard to give his old friend's son a chance at some good pickings. I try to argue with the old fucker, he'll twist my words till he gets me to convince myself that I ought to be grateful for him jumping my claim. Well, hell, the main thing is to get it squared off. Comes down to it, thing to keep in mind is that Pilchard's a one-time proposition, for Doc or for me, and Doc and I go back a long ways, and we'll be running into each other all the time so long's we go on working the frontier, till one or the other of us joins the silent majority.

The breakfast Mrs. Pyle had forced on him was making him bulge against the waistband of his trousers and his vest. The Reid's made a painful impact on him, inside the now skin-tight vest, and he withdrew it and slipped it into a side pocket of his long coat.

He had not realized he was eating as much as he had, being preoccupied, and perhaps influenced, by the amount of food that Holly O'Devie had been putting away. A heaping bowl of oatmeal awash in cream had gone in record time, slices of ham had been rolled up on her fork and devoured whole, and a generous portion of home-fried potatoes—one dish Faro had managed to avoid—had vanished like a snowbank next to a bonfire. At least this morning she had seemed friendlier than the night before, flashing him a wicked grin with a mouth distended with part of the extra-substantial meal she was taking in, and the hint of a wink. Maybe she's got to be fed up pretty solid before her memory gets to working, he thought.

Broken-open crates leaning against the wall marked the shed where Major Mordaunt was conducting his business. Faro went around the side and peered into the shadowy interior. At the far end, a roughly dressed stocky man was bent over a tangle of metal, assembling a spoked wheel onto a tubular frame, his back to Faro. Doc Prentiss was lounging against the wall, surveying the labors of his assistant through the smoke of a fat cigar and studying a sheet of paper which contained several drawings of loop-handled cups in cross-section.

"Major," Faro said.

"Ah, Blake," Doc said. "Morning." A clang came from the end of the shed as the mechanic dropped the framework onto a heap of gears and chains, then stooped to pick it up.

"So it is," Faro said. "Listen, I better have a word or so with you, Major."

"Always glad of that, Mr. Blake," Doc said, with more cheerfulness than Faro had expected. "Let's step out into the sunshine and conduct our business in God's good fresh air. Every breath is a double eagle in the bank of health," he said, drawing deeply on the cigar. "Almost finished with that one, Hayes?" he called.

A grunt from the back of the shed seemed to indicate an affirmative answer. "Sterling fellow, a lucky find," Doc told Faro as they moved out of the mechanic's earshot and leaned against the outer wall of the shed. "A distant cousin of the President, as he tells me, though I'd say he was something of a black sheep in the family, but no matter. He's a dab hand at putting the machines together and making them run, which is something beyond the competence of Major Mordaunt, I can tell you. No direct experience, but one look at the manuals and he was at it. A stroke of luck that he should turn up in this out-of-the-way place just when I needed him. Now, my boy, what was this matter you wished a word about?"

"Well . . ." Faro said. "Look, Doc, you and me, it don't do for us to come up against each other like this. But I don't aim to back off, and I guess neither do you. So—"

"Damn!" Doc said, looking at his watch. "I promised to deliver a machine to some fellow by ten this morning, and it's quarter past now. Just a minute." He stepped back into the shed, and Faro followed. "Hayes!" he called. "Is the cycle for Wilson ready yet?"

"Urr, Major," the mechanic said, facing away from them.

"Damn it, man, is that yes or no?" Doc snapped. "What are you playing at? Is it ready or isn't it?"

He advanced on his employee, with Faro following

after. Doc reached out and took the man by the shoulder, turning him to face forward. "Now, Hayes—"

Faro registered a plump whiskery face, a beaky nose and beady eyes—the face, nose and eyes of Turkey Nickerson.

Chapter 7

Turkey Nickerson's alarmed glare and Faro's amazed one met in a mutually charged instant, then Faro's left hand darted for the Reid's in his vest pocket.

Nickerson gave a shrill, gobbling cry, lowered his head and butted Faro in the midriff. Faro was driven backward onto the earth floor of the shed, still scrabbling in his vest pocket.

Nickerson vaulted onto a bicycle leaning against the back wall, drove his left foot downward powerfully on the pedal and wobbled toward Doc, who quickly stepped aside. "Stop him, Doc!" Faro called, now remembering where he had put the Reid's and digging in the side pocket of his coat.

"What with?" Doc said.

"Your . . . nemmine, Doc." Faro, now on his feet, reached through the bottom of his pocket, discovering a hole in it that had let the pistol fall through and down into the lining. There's a damn thing, he thought. A man that's in a line of work like me don't have no business getting involved with a woman steady-like, but things like this show you you need a steady-like woman to do for you.

By the time he retrieved it and went outside, Nickerson was visible only as a cloud of dust heading west out of Durgin and into the flatlands beyond.

"What was all that about?" Doc wanted to know. "It's pretty low of you, young Faro, to run my mechanic out of town, just because we've had a business disagreement."

"Not that, Doc," Faro said. "Thass Turkey Nickerson, him I tole you of last time we met, the one that wanted me to hire on with him to rob banks or what, me having the gentlemanly appearance that'd let me damp suspicions till the rest of the gang was into the place and scooping up the gelt. And when that didn't work, he had a couple of tries at corpsing me. And I would admire to know how you and him are hooked up."

"Um." Doc stroked his chin. "Fortuitous, my dear boy, purely fortuitous. This Hayes, as he called himself, appeared in town a few days ago, applying for casual work. It appeared that he had been employed in a sewing machine factory as a mechanic, and, as many of the mechanical principles of those machines and mine are the same—indeed, Macduff was once a manufacturer of such domestic instruments before going into the transportation line—I snapped him up. Nickerson, you say. Well, well."

"Gone now, anyhow," Faro said. "Last I heard, he was in the Territorial pen up in Idaho, doing a long term."

"Doubtless he felt it convenient to leave when he saw the opportunity, just as he did now," Doc said.

"Well, hell, Doc," Faro said, "how about we get on

down to the sheriff or the marshal or the head constable or whatever they got here in Durgin, and let him know there's a certified badman and escaper out here in the sands?"

Doc shook his head. "It would be damaging to my operation to go to the law with word that I had hired a known criminal to service my machines. 'If the major doesn't know a crook from an honest man, why should we trust him to know about bicycles?' will be the tenor of thought. Illogical, I grant you, but if everyone was logical, where would the marks come from? Also, if the information originates from you, as the only one hereabouts to know this rogue fowl by sight, other questions, vexatious to you, my boy, would arise, such as the circumstances under which you came to know him. And those questions could well exercise a chilling effect on the reception of your enterprise as well as my own."

Faro, still peering at the tiny smudge on the horizon that marked Turkey Nickerson's passage, turned and looked at Doc sharply. "How come this concern for my enterprisings?" he asked. "Last we talked, Doc, you was claiming a clear track, and all pedestrians, cattle and Faro Blakes best out of the way if they didn't want to get chopped up by the driving wheels."

"Ah, well." Doc shrugged. "Short of appealing to your better nature, there was no way I could come out on top in that. And it seemed to me that that was a sucker bet. I could put a spoke in your wheel, sure enough; but so could you in mine—and nobody would come out ahead. And being ahead is why we're doing what we're doing, my boy. So I thought about it a bit in the long reaches of the night, and it came to me that the big problem was not Polk Pilchard's resources, which are ample enough to enrich us both, but his attitude toward them. He wants what you can give him, he wants what I can give him—in each case, reputation and money. Instead of putting the poor fellow in the place of Aesop's ass, that starved because it couldn't decide which of two bundles of hay to go for first, it seemed to me best that he goes for both propositions at the same time. He can afford it, or thinks he can, and the thing is to make him see it that way."

"And . . ." Faro said.

"Major Mordaunt, Colonel Rowayton, Chief Spotted Tail and all the rest of them have made themselves and me a good living since the Jackson administration by making people see things the way I wanted them to," Doc said. "With the help of a trusted associate, I don't see that handling one Polk Pilchard should give us any problems. And in addition, dear boy," Doc said, looking at Faro fondly, "considering what has passed between us since your youth, I couldn't bear to think what would happen to you if you had me for an enemy."

Chapter 8

"I declare, Major," Mrs. Pyle said, "I never thought about that."

"Few have, dear lady," Doc said. "But I was there, and saw the whole tragic business. The gallant Six Hundred, riding into the fire of the Russian guns at Balaclava, and so few of them returning. As I pointed out, had they been mounted on bicycles of the Macduff type—alas, not then yet invented—the outcome might well have been different."

At lunch, the first meal during Faro's stay at which he had been present, Doc was holding the boarders' rapt attention—with the exception of Holly O'Devie's, which was firmly fixed on the deep bowl of stew which she had maneuvered in front of her—with his accounts of his military experience and how it might have been altered by the bicycle. "I tell you, ladies and gentlemen, with the telegraph, the bicycle and the rapid-fire gun, the very face of warfare is changing. Speed of movement, speed of communication and volume of fire will make the agonizing long-drawn-out bloodletting of war a thing of the past. Disputes of the future will be sharp and short, with four-year campaigns like that of your Civil War an impossibility."

"Would make for some interesting statues, Major," Faro said. "A general or what set up in a park, looking stern at the citizenry, taking hold of the handlebars and saddle of his trusty steed."

"An amusing observation, my dear Blake," Doc said. "Perhaps a little frivolous, but that's all very well from someone who's involved in the good work. Yes, Mrs. Pyle," he said, turning to the landlady, whose eyebrows had risen questioningly, "I have the pleasure to inform you that Mr. Blake, here, has consented to associate himself with my enterprise in addition to his own."

Holly O'Devie, her jaws working on the latest fork- ful of stew, looked at Faro with cool curiosity, but none of the friendly air of complicity she had displayed at breakfast. Most changeable woman I ever been with, he thought.

"I wonder," Doc went on, "if Mr. Blake and I might have the use of the parlor for coffee after our repast, as we have some business matters to discuss."

"Of course, Major," Mrs. Pyle said. "I'll have the girl set it out there, soon's we're done. My, that'll be nice, two of my boarders in together on such big doings. Expect you'll have all the men in Durgin on wheels before long."

"And the ladies too, ma'am," Doc said. "The Mac- duff machines feature the detachable front bar, allow- ing each and every cycle to be converted for the use of the fair sex, the removal accommodating all skirts except for the old-fashioned hoop. No, the Macduff people look forward, not back, and will not countenance the denial of the benefits of increased mobility and health by reason of gender or fashion."

Mrs. Pyle's coffee was the one blot on her cuisine. But diluting it with about an equal amount of bourbon from his flask made it reasonably potable, Faro found.

"You keep coming on about them cycles," he said to Doc as they sat in Mrs. Pyle's "company" parlor over their enhanced coffee, "but this crowd ain't real customers for such, and you ain't really in that trade anyhow. How come you keep at it?"

"Because it's what Major Mordaunt would do, young Faro," Doc said. "Major Mordaunt is an ex-military man, and a fanatic on cycling and what it will mean for the future. Major Mordaunt could no more not talk up cycles than not breathe. And while I'm Major Mordaunt, that's what I'll do."

He took a gulp of his coffee-and-whiskey mixture, shuddered briefly and continued. "As the Bard—or Swan, if you prefer, though where swans come into it I haven't the least idea, they being vicious and stupid fowls—of Avon said, 'One man in his time plays many parts.'"

"That Shakespeare man you used to drum into me wrote something that sounded like that, too, I recollect," Faro said.

"Well, yes," Doc said after a brief pause. "At any rate, the thing in playing a part is to live it. Hilary Mordaunt is no mere mask for me, young Faro, but as it were a second skin. While I'm him, I think Mordaunt, talk Mordaunt and act Mordaunt. I expect you do the same thing, too, though you may not think you're doing it—say, when you're out to bed a prime woman, you figure what it is she wants in a man and see to it that, for the moment, you are that kind of man, rough where she wants it rough, tender along the same lines or whatever. And you are that man, just then, without much art or lying into it."

"I guess so," Faro said. "Though I'm not sure just what kind of part I'm playing in all this stuff, what with being your new partner and all."

"You're my left flank," Doc said. "You sweep around Pilchard's center and bore in with the idea that the cycle race can mesh with the big poker game he's so hot on—the out-of-town sports will relish it as an extra diversion while they're here in Durgin. And I'll work the same line from my end. Between the two of us, we'll have him begging us to turn out his pockets, then hold him upside down by the heels and shake out any leftover coin."

"I talk up the cycles and you talk up the poker, is that it?" Faro asked.

"Exactly so. And if we do it right, we'll lick the platter clean, my boy, just the way Miss Holly handled that stew at lunch." Doc looked at his watch. "In fact, you might as well get at it now, step on over to Pilchard's place and start pitching to him, get in something about Bet-a-Million Gates being known to be a charter member of the League of American Wheelmen."

Faro was surprised. "Is he?"

"Almost certainly not, but Pilchard won't know that, will he? If you tell a man something he has absolutely no way of checking on, it hardly counts as a lie, to my way of thinking."

As Faro raised and dropped the brass knocker on Pilchard's door, he wondered uneasily if Doc's plan made sense. Maybe, if he did a good enough job of persuading Pilchard that the bicycle competition was a good idea, that might just make it sure that he would go for that and not the epic poker game. But, no, Doc wouldn't con his oldest friend into going out and cutting his own throat for Doc's benefit, would he?

Waiting for the door to open, Faro wished he felt a little more certain on that point.

"Oh—Mr. Blake." Amelia Pilchard stood behind the door and looked at him.

"Yes, ma'am," Faro said. "Come by hoping Mr. Pilchard could spare me a minute or so."

"Well . . . he's not in, afternoons. He goes down to an office he has on Front Street, near the hotel, and tends to his investments."

"Oh," Faro said. "Maybe I'd best get on down there and see can I get my minute or what out of him."

"Well, yes. But . . . I'm just about to make myself a pot of tea—it's the girl's afternoon off, so I have to see to it myself. Would you like . . . do you care for tea?"

About as much as jack-rabbit piss, Faro said silently. But it's against my principles to turn down whatever is offered by a first-class woman like this. "A pleasure to have that kind of refreshment, this time of the day, ma'am," he said.

"Cream or lemon?" Mrs. Pilchard asked. Thick drapes pulled across the front window left the parlor in deep shade, and the gleam of the porcelain pot and cups—and of Mrs. Pilchard's pale flesh, seen below her half-length sleeves and above the neckline of her dress—were the chief accents of light in the room. As much as it had two days ago, it reminded Faro of a really expensive whorehouse, and Mrs. Pilchard, once again, seemed to fit in. When not expecting company, she appeared to favor something less elegant than the velvet gown she had worn at lunch and was clad in a loose cotton housedress. It was looser at the top than elsewhere, he noted, as she leaned to pour the tea and the neckline dipped outward, disclosing more than she was probably aware of of the upper slopes of her breasts. She seemed a little more substantial about the middle than she had been on his previous visit, and he supposed that she had dispensed with her stays, though the slight swaying under the top of her dress was evidence enough of that.

With some difficulty, he wrenched his mind back to consider the question she had asked. "Lemon, thanks." Ever since Whitey Porlock, a three-card monte thrower noted for his aversion to strong drink and his addiction to milk, had taken a drink of the stuff during high summer in east Texas, and died writhing a day later, it had been Faro's policy to avoid dairy products.

"One lump or two?"

"Of . . . oh, uh, two, please." Mrs. Pilchard took a pair of silver tongs from the tray on the table between them and lifted two cubes of sugar into Faro's cup and one into her own.

"Oh, darn," she said. "I've got some little cakes in the kitchen and I forgot to bring them out. When the girl's out for her afternoon, I'm on my own and I don't know how to manage. I'll just go get them."

After Amelia Pilchard left the room, Faro sipped his tea. The lemon and sugar had improved it, if jack-rabbit piss flavored with lemon and sugar was any real improvement over straight jack-rabbit piss. He felt in the side pocket of his jacket where his flask rested, fetched it out and added a dollop of bourbon to his cup. After a moment's reflection, he did the same for Mrs. Pilchard's tea. He sipped at his cup and decided that

the brew now had enough bite to it to make it worthwhile drinking.

"Here I am back," Mrs. Pilchard said unnecessarily
as she entered, carrying a small tray heaped with
pastries. "This is finger food, so help yourself; this is
informal, so we don't have to be all dainty, with forks
and such."

Faro bit into a cake that spurted a creamy filling into
his mouth and watched Amelia Pilchard do the same.
He imagined her experiencing the sensation, just as he
was, and wondered if it was having the same effect on
her; no telling quite why, but the old Adam was rising
in him and pressing against the front of his trousers.

She took a sip of her tea and her eyes widened
slightly. "That must have steeped longer than I
thought," she said. "Is it too strong for you?"

"Stronger the tea, the better, my experience," Faro
said solemnly. If the lady didn't know her brew had
been spiked, and wasn't relishing it, he would pour out
the remaining contents of the flask and chew it up.

"Most things are better when they're strong as can
be, Mr. Blake," Amelia Pilchard said. "Tea, horses,
men."

"Women too, ma'am," Faro said.

Amelia Pilchard shrugged, setting up a sideways
quiver under the top of her dress that lasted a full two
seconds after the gesture was completed. "Women
aren't supposed to be strong, Mr. Blake. At least not
when they're married and well-off. A woman married
to a rich man, why, she's not much more than an
ornament, with nothing much going on to make use of
what she is and what she can do."

"Well," Faro said carefully, "a man that's rich is still
a man, and a man that's . . . well, a man, so to
speak . . . he'll appreciate a woman that's strong,
seems to me."

"Some men, maybe," Amelia Pilchard said. "I personally wouldn't know. That was bourbon you put in here, wasn't it?"

"Uh, yes."

"I expect you figured that if you put some liquor in my tea, you could get me tiddly and work your will with me, me being married to a man that doesn't have much will to work anymore, is that it?"

Faro tried to think of any possible answer but the truth to this blunt question and gave up. "Uh, yes."

Mrs. Pilchard drained her cup. "I don't expect it was needed, but it sort of helps, gets me a little warm here and there, and sort of not caring much about things. I marked you down when you were here for lunch, Mr. Blake, and I told myself, there's a man that has some notion about what to do with Amelia Pilchard, and that it wouldn't be too many days before he'll make some excuse to come around and try it out. Pilchard never showed you the upstairs the other day—you want to have a look at it?"

"Uh, yes."

"Oh, my," Mrs. Pilchard said. "So long, so strong . . ." She took Faro's erection in her hands and guided it to her lips. Her sharp teeth nibbled gently at the head; then she moved downward and licked carefully at the shaft and root, chewing softly at the thicket of hair around it. "Hold still a bit." She shifted under him and moved until his swollen penis lay between her breasts, which she pressed together until he was enfolded between them in a warm, dry softness. Her nipples were puckered and swollen, and she stared at him with an unfocused wildness.

She slid up and down against him; the soft skin moved easily, with an arid friction that was pleasant but not stimulating beyond what was needed to maintain his erection.

"Don't . . ." she said.

"Don't what?"

"Let yourself . . . you know. I don't want . . . it'd be a waste, just now. I like this, oh, I like it, but . . . I want more, so much more."

Faro reached down between his spread legs and felt for Amelia Pilchard's smooth, rounded belly, and below. "Thass where I figure to let myself, comes the time for it," he said. "Oh, and ain't you just ready, Lord 'a' mercy." His fingers probed the wiry tangle, then behind it, sliding in the mossy moistness.

Amelia Pilchard gave a throaty grunt and convulsed under him. Faro slid one finger in, then another, searching out her inwardness, learning new contours. Damned strange, every woman was mostly the same arrangement inside, but each one had something different about her, and no mistaking any one for any other, that way. Something surged against his fingers, and Amelia Pilchard gave a sharp indrawn cry.

She arched upward and took him into her mouth, moistening him to full slickness, then reached for his shoulders and pushed downward. Faro eeled down her body and thrust into her as her legs scissored apart, driving deeply into where his fingers, still pungent with her scent, had just been. Again, he felt her surge, and now she seemed to be shaken with an interior tide that sent a rush of rosy color to her face and chest; she gave a high plaintive call that reminded him of the gulls he had seen, once, wheeling over the Great Salt Lake.

Seagulls had no erotic associations for him, but all the same Faro felt the familiar sense of focusing and tension calling for release, then the release itself, spasming into Mrs. Pilchard, feeling himself filling her.

He lay atop her for a moment, then moved aside as he felt himself begin to dwindle. He was warm all over, except where the lightly stirring afternoon air cooled his damp quiescent penis.

"Umm," Mrs. Pilchard purred. "Nice."

"Indeedy," Faro said. "About the nicest."

"Now the next is," Mrs. Pilchard said, "I'm sort of kneeling, while you come at me from behind, so you can play with my bubs while you're doing me."

"Next?" Faro said. "Listen, ma'am, that what we done about used me up for a while. Doing ain't in the cards just now."

"No?" Mrs. Pilchard said. Sharp fingernails moved along the underside of Faro's penis. The first strokes were no more than an inch and a half; the fifth and sixth had another inch to cover; later ones, four inches, then six, then . . .

"Agh!" Amelia Pilchard said as Faro drove into her, cushioned on her full buttocks, his fingers kneading her dangling breasts and flicking her swollen nipples.

Faro looked blankly at his clothes scattered on the bedroom floor and wondered how they would fit when he put them back on. It seemed to him that he would have to snug his belt in at least four notches to keep his trousers from falling down around his ankles, and that his coat would hang on him in folds, like an opera cloak. If the fit took him and Mrs. Pilchard to go at it again, it seemed to him that there wouldn't be much left of them at the end of it but skin and bones.

The idea of getting up, picking up his drawers and pulling them on, then the trousers, then the shirt, then the socks, then the shoes, then the tie, then the coat, seemed too effortful to contemplate for the moment. Faro let his gaze wander around the richly furnished

bedroom, vaguely taking in the details of chairs, cabi-
nets, lamps, wallpaper, pictures. . . .

"Hey," he said to Amelia Pilchard, who was lying
next to him and looking at the carved furbelows on the
ceiling with an expression of deep contentment. "What
you got most of along the walls here is oil paintings
of countrysides and cows and scenes from the Bible
until Hell wouldn't have it. Whass that thing over
there?"

He pointed at a large framed sepia-tinted photograph
of a huddle of derelict buildings surrounded by heaps of
fragmented rocks.

"Oh. The Good Indian mine," Amelia Pilchard said.
"That's Mr. Pilchard's fun—about the only kind he has.
When it ran out, and everybody left the camp, it turned
into a ghost town, and that was when he put it off on
that McTeague, that was his partner, and sold it to him
as if it was worth something, when it wasn't. So he
made all his money on it, first out of the mine, when it
was producing, then when he cheated his partner with
it. And he had a photographer come by and make a
picture of it for him, for a reminder of how sharp he
was. Uses it to hide the door of the safe he keeps all his
money in, right there. Mr. Pilchard doesn't believe in
banks, says he likes to have his cash where he can get at
it when he wants it. Mr. Pilchard likes to have everything where he can use it, though he doesn't use much
of anything he has a lot of."

Amelia Pilchard sat up on the rumpled bed and
looked morosely at the photograph on the wall. "You
know, he could have had all the money he cared to
spend if he'd just worked the mine and let McTeague
know when it petered out. But it pleasured him to
hoodwink his partner and make some more that way,
and leave nothing behind but a ghost town out there in

the hills. That's why he's tickled to have that picture up there in front of the safe."

Faro pulled his drawers from the floor and inserted his feet into them, then hoisted them into place. Doc's always saying you can't cheat an honest man, he reflected. Looks like we got us a prime candidate for cheating in this Pilchard, all right.

Chapter 9

Swallowing a mouthful of Mrs. Pyle's coffee with three spoons of sugar to make it drinkable, Faro considered the old saw about lucky at cards, unlucky at love. Pilchard certainly bore that out. He had done almighty well at Callahan's last night, and, for the other end of it, there was what had happened with Faro and Mrs. Pilchard in the afternoon. On the other hand, Faro wondered if having his wife thoroughly covered by another man in the afternoon would count as bad luck to Pilchard. A man that didn't relish what he had waiting around the house probably didn't know or care what he was missing out on or who had the use of it.

"Beautiful day," Holly O'Devie said, swallowing a mouthful of grits and clearing her plate of the last traces of red-eye gravy with a slab of bread.

"So it is," Doc said heartily. "Old Sol doing what he can to reduce everything to adobe, not a cloud in the sky, and even a soft breeze to cut the bite of the sun's rays. Might I have another cup of coffee, Mrs. P.?"

"I've got a fancy for a ride outside of town," Holly O'Devie said, once she had attacked and conquered the gravy-sodden bread. "Out in California, I used to get out in the country a lot, and I haven't yet seen what things are like around here. There's that old mining town, out a few miles. It might be interesting to see what that's like."

"It would be my pride and pleasure to offer you the complimentary use of one of Macduff's best cycles for the excursion," Doc said. "A smooth ride, very nearly effortless so long as you keep to comparatively level ground, and no danger whatever of runaways. Our solid tires, of the best grade of South American rubber, eliminate many of the jolts of the roadway, which at their worst are easier on the, ah, frame than the gait of the saddle horse."

"Well, I'm used to horses, Major," Holly O'Devie said, "which is more than I can say about bicycles. I'll rent one at the livery and amble around for a while. Say, Mrs. Pyle, as I won't be in for lunch, d'you think I could have some sandwiches made up to take with me?"

"Surely, dear," the landlady said. "There's some cold lamb, beef and ham. What would you like?"

"Two of each," Holly O'Devie said.

"Oh, Doc," Faro said reproachfully. "That amounts to triple-dipping me in shit and hanging me up to dry. I mean, I can take apart my Reid's and clean it, or do what's needed to a dealing box so's it'll put out the card I want, but I ain't no bicycle mechanic. I didn't bargain any time for nothing like that."

"Face it, my boy," Doc said, "we need to get these

machines together and in working order if there's to be a race, let alone the sales we need. And you have to admit that it was your irruption onto these premises that cost me the services of my assistant. The Macduff people have prepared an excellent manual and provided an armamentarium of tools and lubricants, so that for men of your and my native intelligence the task should be child's play."

Faro clenched his teeth and surveyed the litter of half-assembled bicycles that Turkey Nickerson had left behind, then accepted the inevitable and approached the job of getting them in roadworthy condition.

Half an hour later, he called to Doc, "You got any children you want to bring in on this? If it's a snap for them, like you say, I could use the help." There was a tear in the right sleeve of his shirt, areas of skin absent from his knuckles and smears of grease on his shirtfront and trousers. "Thisyer chain, it's like some damn rattlesnake; every time I get it in place, it kind of jumps at me and bites me whenas I try to tighten it."

"The thing is to slide it onto drive wheel A before you put it onto the rear cogwheel H. Very simple once you shit, shit, shit," Doc said, as the handlebar he was installing suddenly slid into place, mashing two of his fingers.

"If Turkey Nickerson was to walk in here just now, I believe I would welcome him as a man and brother," Faro said. "Anybody that can put these things together and make them run and not get his anatomy chewed up has my respect. I swear to God, Doc, this chain is about two links shy of what it needs to be to fit onto the fucking cogs or whatever they are unless I bend the whole damn frame like a bow."

"From what we saw of him last, I doubt Master Nickerson will be back," Doc said. "He seemed particularly anxious not to renew your acquaintance."

"I guess because of me having a shooter on me, and him not caring to use his own so close in to town. They'd of had a posse after him in about no time once the shots was heard and they found you and me all shot to pieces, and I don't expect these things could outrun some fast horses."

"On level terrain and in the hands of an expert, it could be a contest," Doc said. "Now, there's the really sore point—the rascal made off with the one of my machines that's in the best working order, and I haven't the least idea where he's gone to. I confess I never bothered to learn the location of his doubtless squalid lodgings. I just signed him on after a talk at Callahan's and told him to show up here."

"Was he to of turned right after he got out of town and kept going," Faro said, "wouldn't be too many days before he was at the Grand Canyon, and with any luck the brake wouldn't work and he'd pedal right into it. Or we could have a Wanted poster put out on him. Wonder if we could make the law see it that a man ought to hang as much for stealing a fellow's bicycle as his horse?"

"They couldn't do it in the traditional way of rough Western justice," Doc said, tightening a nut on the handlebar, then loosening it and adjusting the bar to a rakish angle that he seemed to prefer. "Imagine the scene, young Faro. The malefactor surrounded by the avenging vigilantes, blindfolded and secured to the limb of a convenient cottonwood by a length of hemp, astride the vehicle he has purloined. One last statement of the indictment, a perfunctory 'May God have mercy on your soul,' though the devout among the crowd would as soon see him on the eternal griddle, and then one amongst them gives the innocent machine a hard push on the rear wheel, speeding it from under him. And as it wobbles ahead and falls to the ground, there the fucker is, standing up, with the noose loose around his neck. They'd have to wrestle him to the ground to stretch him."

It was something past noon before Doc declared that they had done all that reasonable men could be expected to accomplish in a day's manual labor, and that it was time to relax into the pleasures of civilization again, such as getting outside some of the best refreshments that the Butler House Hotel offered.

"Mrs. Pyle sets a hearty and tasty table," he said, "but I have a fancy for something more on the stylish side. Also, at the Butler House, lunch can be accompanied by any variety of stimulating fluids, whereas Ma Pyle runs to coffee or lemonade, with tea provided for the high livers on special order. I believe I have ingested about two drams of axle grease in the course of the morning, and it's well known that alcohol is the best solvent for such substances."

"Also good applied externally for abrasions, contusions and scrapes, so I heared," Faro said.

"A sinful waste," Doc said, inspecting his bruised fingers. "The thing is, get enough of the stuff inside you, and you don't notice what the outside feels like."

The luncheon menu at the Butler House was probably quite good, Faro thought. But when he and Doc had finished whatever it was they had ordered, he had no clear idea of what it had been. Once they had taken aboard enough bourbon (for Faro) and port, rye and champagne (for Doc) to wipe out the recollection of their morning's toil, what they had eaten (he was pretty sure they had eaten something) was beyond his recall.

"Gives a man a feeling of satisfaction," Doc said.

"What does?"

"Solid work—putting stuff together, making it work."

"No, it don't," Faro said.

Doc looked at the bubbles that rose to the surface of his glass and said, "Well, no, it doesn't. Only thing, it's got to be done if the really good stuff's to be pulled off, d'you see? Like you practicing bottom deals and so on, or me studying out all the angles to a scam, so as to get what we want to going. Tedious, trying, but there it is."

"At least you ain't got us doing demonstrations of the sons of bitches," Faro said. "You might be a dab hand at putting them machines together, but I guess it'd be beyond you to show the marks how you can scorch along on 'em."

"You think so?" Doc asked. "Let me remind you, young Faro, that snow on the roof doesn't mean that the fire on the hearth has gone out. Traveling as I occasionally do in salubrious tonics, fit for man or beast as the occasion or the customer calls for, I make it a point to be up on the health requirements of my corpus, and to see to it that I maintain my natural vigor unimpaired." He drained his glass of most of its champagne and poured the remnants of the port bottle into it.

"Now you," he went on, "despite the fact that you can spot me a brace of decades—"

"Three of 'em, Doc," Faro said.

"—or so, haven't taken care of yourself. Those vile cheroots, like the one you're just lighting, your late hours, your exclusive preference for the grain rather than the grape, your indulgence of your . . . other appetites—"

"I do like humping, yeah," Faro said. "But what's—"

"—these excesses drain you, my boy, sap your fiber, diminish your substance, far more than the effects of carefully tended advancing years."

"Well, hell, I guess you could run one of them

machines of yours for twenty miles or what and not even breathe hard, whiles I'd be blown and foundering in the roadway after one, and waiting for someone to come along and put me out of my misery, is that it, Doc?" Faro said, topping up his glass yet again. "Lemme tell you, I don't care above half for settling my fambly jewels onto that lousy little seat and pushing up and down with my legs so's to get to someplace that prob'ly wouldn't be worth the bother of getting to, but I can damn well do anything you can, and not come away from it winded, neither."

Drinking's a thing that a man's going to do if he's got the taste for it, Faro thought, and so is bragging. And there ain't no harm to neither, taken separate. But drinking and bragging at one and the same time, why, that can lead to a man forking a saddle that's built to geld him and pushing a damnfool cogwheel around and around and around, like any turnspit dog, so's he don't fall over sideways and dash his brains out in the road. I as soon give up bragging, the drink being more reliable in the way of comfort and good cheer.

Faro was especially soured by the fact that Doc was well ahead of him on the westward road out of Durgin, and seemed not to be experiencing the difficulties that he himself had in keeping the bicycle upright and moving in the right direction. He drove down hard with his left foot, then his right, and the bicycle surged ahead, pulling out of the wobble that had been troubling him. He got the sense of just when to exert power in the downward strokes and when to let the sole of his boot ride upward, lifted by the pedal, and began to gain on Doc. The forked tails of Doc's old-fashioned frock coat flared out behind him as he pedaled. It seemed to Faro that one of them stuck out stiffly, almost as if it had been starched; maybe the wind was catching it at some odd angle.

This ain't all that bad, and it does get you across the countryside at some clip, and no jolting your bones loose, the way a horse does, he thought. Plus which it won't stray off when you light down from it, nor it won't turn and bite at you when it takes a notion, nor yet drop a bushel of shit behind it when you're sashaying along and stop to raise your hat to a lady. And no rubbing it down after a run, either. And, being as the cycle's made of iron, steel, leather and rubber, it's prob'ly got a lot more brains than a horse, too.

Somehow, after the first mile, he seemed to have command of the machine and to be able to send it along the level stretch of road as easily as he pleased. His silent, smooth progress was suddenly exhilarating, and the rush of the wind in his face made him feel almost giddily carefree.

"Hey, Doc," he called, drawing almost level with his partner, "I got to say you got something here. S'prised myself, I can get her going like I done. This is about close onto getting to be fun."

"So it is," Doc said. "A pity we'll be getting out of this line once we've plucked Polk Pilchard. There'll be money in plenty to be made by the fellows that stick with it and put in their hours. But that's not for us, eh, my boy?"

"Well, no, it ain't," Faro said. "Hey, there's a kind of dip ahead here. We get onto that, we could really build up a head of speed, I expect, faster'n a horse could do."

Before them, the hard-packed plateau that led away from Durgin angled slightly but perceptibly downward for a distance of about half a mile, then leveled again, going into a slight upgrade just before ending in a group of rocky prominences.

"I haven't tried out Messrs. Macduffs' product on a downslope," Doc said, "and I owe it to the customers to see what happens if I do. Come on, then."

He drove his bicycle down the slope, gathering speed almost instantly. After the first hundred yards, he removed his feet from the whirling pedals and let the machine make its own pace, which constantly increased. Faro followed him, and was himself soon obliged to let the bicycle take over. Wind whipped his face and coat, sending the skirt streaming out behind him. Shit, I misdoubt I ever gone this fast before except on a crack train with a drunk engineer, he thought. Dust spurted into his face, sped there by Doc's whirling wheels alongside of him; he winced as a flung pebble took him in the cheek, but the sensation of speed had made him almost as drunk as the bourbon he had taken at the Butler House, and he paid no attention.

When the speeding bicycles hit level ground, they rolled ahead at almost undiminished velocity for a moment. Faro waited until he sensed a slowing of the forward motion, then reached for the spinning pedals, slamming first one foot and then the other onto each as it came to the top of its cycle, and driving hard with his thigh muscles. He felt the pedals take hold, sending the slowing machine ahead in a powerful surge, and drew level with Doc, then ahead of him.

"Heydee, Doc," Faro called over his shoulder, "ain't I just the scorcher, though, and first time up."

"A credit to my instruction, my boy," Doc said. "But I'll venture that I'll be even with you when we fetch up at wherever it is we're going."

"How about up there, near them hills?" Faro asked. "Not more'n a mile on, and no broken ground to get over before then. Winner gets all he can drink at Callahan's tonight."

"You're on," Doc said. "Whoever's ahead when we get to that shack just at the bottom of that first hill on the left scoops the pot."

Faro pumped at the pedals, feeling the machine move ahead under him, and headed for the building Doc had indicated. As he neared it at the dizzying speed the bicycle built up on the hard-packed nearly level earth, it and its derelict companions suddenly fell into a familiar configuration—they were the remnants of the town that had briefly grown up about the Good Indian mine, as shown in the photograph Polk Pilchard kept in his bedroom, masking his safe.

Hey, this is where that Holly said she was coming out riding today, he thought. Maybe she's still hereabouts. Nice to see her, though it'd be nicer if Doc wasn't along.

Faro's front wheel crunched first against the heap of rock tailings that lay at the foot of the hill and in front of the abandoned buildings. Seconds later, Doc came up to him. They dismounted and Doc said, "Looks like the drinks are on me."

"Whoof," Faro said. "That is the most effort I put out in some time. But I got to say that it beats going around on some hayburner or coming this distance afoot. Less go up and poke around, see what's left of this place."

"Good enough, now we're here," Doc said. "Any idea what it is or what it used to be?"

Faro explained, though not going into just how he had come to see the photograph of Polk Pilchard's personal ghost town.

"Indeed," Doc said. "It'll be interesting to see the scene of the foundation of Master Pilchard's fortune. I feel it in my bones, boy, we're going to pluck that pigeon down to bare skin."

They wheeled their bicycles up the incline of crushed rock and leaned them against a collapsing building that had once been a shed of some kind.

"This one used to be the store," Doc said, peering into one structure that had a cobwebbed counter and shelves at the far end. "Doubled as the saloon, I'd say," he added, pointing to some shards of broken bottles, the glass fragments still shiny after the passage of years, on the floor.

Their tour of the buildings took little time, and after a few minutes they were approaching the timber-framed mine entrance at the base of the hill. Two rusty pieces of iron spiked to wooden ties, still unrotted in the dry air, led into it. "Rails for the ore car," Doc said. He started forward.

Faro eyed the oblong patch of darkness the timbers outlined. "We really want to go in there, Doc? Ain't nobody been tending it these last dozen years, and nothing to say it won't fall down on our heads."

"It's not my ambition to penetrate the bowels of the earth," Doc said. "But there's no harm in just stepping in and having a look around the entrance."

In this he was incorrect; when he and Faro were six feet past the timber framing and peering around the gloomy cave that had been cut from the rocky hillside, a voice said, "Hold it right there, gents, and move your hands upwards, awful slow and easy."

They turned in the direction the voice had come from and saw a shadowed burly figure. It was indistinct in the near-darkness, but there was enough light to strike a gleam from the two revolvers it held.

Turkey Nickerson had made his second reappearance in Faro's life.

Chapter 10

"For Chrissake, Nickerson," Faro said disgustedly, "whyn't you just keep on going when you run off with the major's cycle? What the fuck are you doing here, anyhow?"

"Arresting trespassers," Turkey Nickerson said, causing Faro to wonder if he, or Nickerson, or both of them, had taken leave of their wits.

"I am the right and proper owner of this here property," Nickerson went on, "with the papers to prove it." He backed away from them a few feet, stuck one revolver into the waistband of his trousers, covering Doc and Faro with the other, and fished out a roll of paper from the side pocket of his greasy sheepskin jacket. "Deed to the Good Indian, all wrote out and proper. It don't mention Turkey Nickerson's name, but to Turkey Nickerson's way of thinking, having a hand on it is what counts. Far's as I'm concerned, it's my property. And you're intruding on it. Got the right to shoot you down like dogs, but that ain't Turkey Nickerson's way of doing things, no, sir." He flourished the revolver he held. "You just move on in a ways ahead of me."

Faro moved into the gloom, with Doc next to him, hoping not to stumble and excite Turkey Nickerson's trigger finger. A wash of light came from in front of them. "Left there," Turkey Nickerson said. They turned and found themselves in a room cut from rock and earth, with a chair and a lit lantern standing on a table.

"My office," Turkey Nickerson said. "But it ain't got accommodation for clients, I'm sorry to say, so you two just stand over against the wall while we have us a talk."

After relieving Faro of his Reid's and patting both him and Doc about the waist and side pockets to make sure neither was carrying another weapon, he sat in the chair, laid the rolled paper on the table and leveled the revolver at them, steadying its butt on the table. "Nice to see you again, Major," he said. "Hey, that's a good one, ain't it? See, you're a major and I'm a miner, or anyhow a mine owner. Kind of a joke, just come to me, but that's how Turkey Nickerson's mind works, quick as a rattrap."

"You're so all-fired anxious for his company, you could of come calling in Durgin," Faro said.

Nickerson shook his head. "No, no, that ain't Turkey Nickerson's way, so it isn't, not to go paying visits where there'd be fellows that know a little too much about where old Turkey's been and what he's done, and where he's supposed to be just now, especially. Was I to have showed up there, it wouldn't have been above the time it takes a cow to let a fart that you'd have been down at the police station, talking about me being wanted back in the Idaho pen, and that wouldn't do, now, would it? But by fortune and accident, here you are, and able to help me out with a problem I got."

"Anything in our power, of course, my dear fellow," Doc said. "You have but to command our assistance."

"I figure so," Turkey Nickerson said, gesturing with the revolver.

"What the fuck do you mean, you own this place?" Faro asked. "Polk Pilchard in Durgin unloaded it onto his partner once it was reamed out of all the gold it had, fellow name of McTeague, what I heard."

Nickerson flattened the paper on the table with one hand and looked at it in the lantern light. "Right, Norris McTeague, of Yerba Seca, Californy, 'bout thirty miles outside San Francisco. That's the former owner, now deceased, and this here paper and so this here mine is mine by right of having tooken hold of it."

"How did that come about?" Doc asked. Faro was well aware that Doc had no interest whatever in Turkey Nickerson's history and exploits, but that he considered that a Nickerson talking about himself, and enjoying the topic, was a Nickerson unlikely to loose off a sudden shot at his captives.

"Now that is a interesting story," Nickerson said. "See, when I bust out of the pen in Idaho, back in March, I headed west, aiming to get as far from Idaho as I could. And, direction I was going, San Francisco's about as far that way as you can go before your hat floats. So I hung around there for a while, and I got to know a couple of fellows that was kind of Turkey Nickerson's sort, game for a few ways to pick up money that didn't call for nothing dangerous unless it was worth it."

He gave Faro a glance of disfavor. "Was I to have had someone like you in my string, there's lots of things I could have done, easier and better paying, since you can pass for a gentleman, almost, and get inside places that'd show the door to Turkey Nickerson, making the work a lot more simple. But, no, you wouldn't take the chance when you had it. Too good for the likes of Turkey Nickerson, that was how you seen it. Well, well, no hard feelings, now that we'll be working together finally."

"How is that?" Faro asked uneasily. His arms were beginning to ache, and he let them drift downward a little, though keeping them well away from his body.

"All in good time. First things first, that's Turkey Nickerson's motto."

As Nickerson told it, he and his associates had found it expedient to leave San Francisco and head for the more rural areas outside it. "I expect hitting three old ladies on the head and taking their purses all in one week, and all in one block on Powell Street, was bound to cause ructions amongst the law and get them nosing around, but that was where it was easiest to get at them, and a man's got to live."

Checking out Yerba Seca for opportunities for the exercise of their craft, Nickerson and his men heard of the McTeague house. Its owner, a substantial merchant and financier, who had died a few months back, had left it richly furnished, and rumor had it that most of his fortune was concealed on the premises. They also learned that the heirs had just left on a theater-and-shopping trip to San Francisco and would be absent for the better part of a week. In the quiet surroundings of Yerba Seca, it was considered an adequate precaution against theft to ask the local constable to keep an eye out for anything out of the ordinary on his nightly rounds. For Turkey Nickerson and his men it had been a simple matter to wait until the lawman had passed, then slip inside the empty house.

"We didn't show no lights, of course," Turkey Nickerson said. "Waited till first light before we set ourselves to having a real good look around. We'd figured to be through and away before sunup."

Doc coughed and fanned the air in front of his face. "A little close in here," he said. Faro glanced at him. Though dank and beginning to smell of coal oil from the lantern, the air was fresh enough. The old bugger's working out something, he thought.

Turkey Nickerson ignored Doc's comment and went on, "Biggest damn house I ever was in, and rigged out like the Palace Hotel for the furniture and what. But there wasn't no jewels in the upstairs rooms, and there wasn't anything in the safe in the big room that was jammed with books except for a couple hundred dollars in greenbacks. The old skinflint must have put it in the bank or someplace, or them that he left it to did. It's a shame the mistrustful natures some people have."

"The deed was in the safe, too, I imagine," Doc said.

Nickerson shook his head. "Nope. Was in a glass frame, hanging on the wall. Looked at it, seen it mentioned a gold mine, so it had to be worth something, and I took it along. It ain't Turkey Nickerson's way to leave behind something that mentions owning gold mines. So I figured, once I had the paper, that was on the way to being Turkey Nickerson's mine."

Irritated at the waste of their time, Nickerson and his men had broken up some of the furniture, emptied the fuel from several lamps onto the fragments of wood and cloth, and set fire to it. "Someone that ain't got the trust in their fellow man to leave their valuables and cash safe in their own home don't deserve soft treatment, to my mind. A lesson to them not to be so greedy, to come back and find the place burned down."

With the house well afire behind them, and its smoke beginning to rise in the early morning air, Nickerson and his men had decamped. Once away from Yerba Seca, he had decided that the best course for them was to head for Arizona and see what could be made of the Good Indian mine. "No problem to get some crook lawyer to do up some kind of transfer papers that'd make the thing look good, after I'd made sure that it was worthwhile. With McTeague out of it, likely I'd have had the working of the mine for a while before them it was left to caught on, and then it would have gone into the courts for maybe years, what with me having the papers, and none but me to say how I come by them, the house being burned down and all. It's Turkey Nickerson's way to think things out, d'you see?"

"But you found in fact that the Good Indian wasn't producing and wouldn't ever produce again," Doc said, following the comment with a rasping gasp.

"Just so," Nickerson said. "But me and the boys, we figured it was at least a place to hole up where we wouldn't be looked for while I studied out what to do, now that we was here."

"Not the best place," Doc said faintly.

"It ain't the Butler House Hotel, no," Nickerson said, "but it ain't Turkey Nickerson's way to complain of rough living for a while."

"Not what I meant," Doc said. "The air . . . you've heard of firedamp?"

"Not to my recollection," Nickerson said.

"Vapors . . . from the depths of the diggings," Doc said. "They replace the good air and leave living creatures with nothing to breathe. In short order, cessation of respiration ensues."

"Which kind of outcomings does whatever that is lead to?" Turkey Nickerson asked uneasily.

"Death," Doc said. "It may be only my fancy, or the parlous state of an old man's lungs, but I am experiencing some difficulty in breathing, and . . . Well, no, I see your lamp is burning a trifle high and smoking the chimney a bit. In the old days, that would have been an infallible sign of the presence of the noxious gases, but now, with the universal employment of Prentiss's Patent Anti-Explosive Admixture by prudent householders, it merely indicates—"

"Hey," Turkey Nickerson said. "That's a plain old lantern, loaded with coal oil, and no patent shitballs into it."

"Then unless you get the chimney off it and turn down the wick, we're all dead men," Doc said. "I have had my turn at bat, so to speak, but it may be that you would prefer to have the use of a few more years in which—"

Turkey Nickerson snatched for the lamp and squealed as the curved glass chimney burned his fingers. Doc bent nearly double, reaching behind him and under his coat. His arm snaked forward, his hand holding a glittering length of metal, which he brought down on Nickerson's right hand, which still held the revolver. Nickerson squealed again, and the weapon dropped from his fingers.

Faro, on the alert ever since Doc had begun his fictitious complaint about the quality of the air in the mine chamber, dove for the rock-strewn floor, took up a loose chunk that almost filled his palm, lunged at Turkey Nickerson and brought the roughly cut stone against his head as hard as he could.

Nickerson fell backward out of his chair and to the floor, and lay still.

Faro dropped the rock and leaned on the table, breathing heavily. "I suppose there ain't nothing in what you said about firedamp?" he asked Doc.

"Perhaps, but it has nothing to do with how things are here," Doc said. "My spiel served its purpose, didn't it?"

"What the hell have you got there?" Faro asked,

looking at the length of thick stiff wire that Doc still held.

"Spare spoke, in case of breakage or bendings," Doc said. "Half a dozen of them, along with a couple of wrenches, back here." He patted the left fork of his claw-hammer coat. "A fellow of Nickerson's background can't be expected to be up on the niceties of good tailoring—specifically, to know that a well-made frock coat has pockets in each tail, unlikely to come to the notice of anyone that's frisking you. Now, young Faro, let's get out of this."

"I'm with you, Doc," Faro said. He grabbed Turkey Nickerson's revolver from the table and started from the chamber. Doc stopped and looked at the spoke in his hand and at the supine Nickerson. "It'd save a lot of trouble," he said, "if I were to stick one end of this over his chest or his eye or some soft spot, and hit the other end a good blow with a rock."

"Less just get out of here, Doc," Faro said.

They stood blinking in the afternoon sun at the mine entrance; Faro was surprised that it was so little lower than it had been when they had entered the timber-framed doorway. "Cycles're over yonder," he said, pointing. "We can—"

"You can hold it right there." Faro and Doc swiveled and turned toward the roughly dressed man who held a shotgun on them from behind the shelter of a rocky outcropping of the hillside.

"Well, you should have known it wouldn't be Turkey Nickerson's way not to have sentries or what, once he's got himself a place to hide out in," Nickerson said. He had no revolver in his hand this time, nor did he require one, since Doc and Faro were securely trussed, hand and foot, and positioned against the rough wall of the room in which he had addressed them before.

Nickerson rubbed his head. "I don't specially rate myself as a storyteller, but I got to admit that it's new to me to have someone cold-cock me sooner'n hear me out. Howsomever, gents, here you are back again, and it's my aim to have my say. Now, best I recollect, I was at where I and the boys came here, and we found that the Good Indian was a dead proposition. Well, we hung around some, and we found that Mr. Polk Pilchard, that'd had all the good out of it, and even cheated his partner to get some more, he was still a live one. Anybody looking to collect some money in or around Durgin, why, he's talking about Polk Pilchard."

Nickerson had satisfied himself that, unlike those concerning his late ex-partner, the rumors that Pilchard kept his personal wealth on his home premises, were accurate. "Heard the banker mourning it over a beer in Callahan's—said it was a sin against nature not to have all them thousands and tens of thousands of dollars out earning two and a half percent interest."

Nickerson had wanted to have a reasonable excuse to be around Durgin while he studied how to loot Polk Pilchard's fortune, and Doc's inquiries had come as a godsend. "Knew no more of bicycles than the chick unhatched," he said. "But when I was in the pen in Idaho, they put me in the laundry, and had me keeping the sewing machines, and I learned all about how they work and how the doojiggers in them fit together. And it seemed to me it was the same thing with the cycles—one thing turns and makes other things move."

"And so it is," Doc said heartily. "I must say, Nickerson—Hayes, if you'd prefer—that you were a first-grade mechanic. It may interest you to know, in fact, that the Macduff company constructed sewing machines before turning to bicycles."

"Well, it don't," Nickerson said. "Anyhow, when you come in the other morning, Blake, it was a shock to me, and I took off out here till I could figure out what to do about that, and about what I was after with this Polk Pilchard. And now it all comes clear to me."

"How is that?" Doc asked.

Nickerson smiled at them. "Why, I will untie you and Blake, and send you on back to Durgin. And you will find out just where Pilchard keeps his money, find out when's the best time to go in after it and get it, and lend me and the boys a hand in the getting."

"Why would we do that?" Doc asked.

"Yeah," Faro added, wondering if he were signing his death warrant, "if you was to let us go on back to Durgin, what's to keep us from setting the law onto you?"

"The fact that I'd spot anybody coming a long way off, and make my dispositions, for one thing," Turkey Nickerson said. "So it would be damned hard to smoke me out, that kind of advance notice. Plus which I'd have time to do things it'd shame me to talk about to the lady before me and the boys take off and leave her dead or worse. And considering the nice things she says about you and the major, I don't expect you'd care much for that."

Turkey Nickerson called over his shoulder, "Okay, Mike."

From around a corner of the corridor, the third of Nickerson's henchmen pushed the stumbling, bound figure of Holly O'Devie.

Chapter 11

Holly O'Devie's eyes rolled at them over the dirty red handkerchief that bound her mouth. "She's not talking on them topics as much now," Turkey Nickerson said, "as she took to shouting and yelling when she seen as we meant to keep her here for a spell, and I got tired of hearing her, and didn't want any chance comers to do the same, so she got gagged. Take her back, Mike."

Mike dragged the struggling Holly back around the corner, and both of them disappeared from Faro and Doc's sight. Faro wondered if she had had a chance to eat the four sandwiches she had had Mrs. Pyle make up; if not, she would be pretty hungry about now, the way she ate.

"Why did you grab that girl?" Doc asked.

Nickerson shrugged. "She come out here, might have been snooping, so I went and made some palaver with her, said I was kind of squatting out here. Mentioned she was boarding with you and Blake, here, and

107

the thought come to me that I could use her some way, so I knocked her down and had the boys rope her up. What I had in mind, I'd get word to you about that and suggest you come in with me on getting out of this Pilchard what I aim to. But it turned out," he went on, "that I didn't have to go to no trouble of that sort, no, sir, here you come straight into my parlor. Well, Turkey Nickerson ain't the man to throw back any bread that's cast on the waters to him, so he ain't, and so here you are."

He rubbed the side of his head, where a purple mark was appearing under the mat of hair above his ear. "I don't grudge you fellows your high spirits none, and it's useful for me to know about that business with the pockets in your tail coat, Major, so's I won't be taken unawares again that way. The main thing is, you see, I got to have your help, and you got to give it to me."

"Well, we don't," Faro said. "You can keep us here, long's you got us tied, or you can turn us loose. That about your doing bad stuff to Miss O'Devie, that's just bluff and you know it."

Nickerson looked at him for a few seconds, then turned and called over his shoulder, "Mike! Take the young lady's gag off, then do that first thing you told me you was thinking of."

Faro heard Holly O'Devie's shrill yell of indignation as the gag came off, then a choked, bubbling howl. "So you ain't bluffing," Faro said hastily. "I guess we can talk."

"Mike!" Nickerson called again. "Lay off that."

"Aw, Turkey! Before I—"

"Yeah, before that. Stop it and get the gag back in. Expect she'll be glad of it by now."

The noises from around the corner stopped, and Faro breathed more easily.

"Ah," Doc said. "Just what is it you want of us?"

"About everything," Nickerson said. "You're in the town, and you've got the ear of this Polk Pilchard. I want to know where he keeps his cash—and I know it's in his house, so don't try to give me any hogwash about it being banked somewheres in St. Louis or Flagstaff or places like them. And I want to know what kind of place it's in, likely a safe, and what kind of safe it is. And I want to know when Polk Pilchard and Mrs. Polk Pilchard ain't likely to be in the house or, at the worst, not in that chunk of the house where the money is. And I want all that by not much after this time tomorrow— say about sunset. One or two of you come on out here with all that and Mike don't get turned loose on the lady. We keep her until we've gone in and got it, and then you're welcome to come out and turn her loose, 'cause me and the boys will be long gone."

Turkey Nickerson looked at them coldly. "And if you got any ideas about reception parties or what when we come after Polk Pilchard's money, forget them. Me and Ben will be enough for that, and Mike'll be here with the young lady. We don't come back when I tell him we will, he'll do what he's a mind to, then take off. And after Mike's done what he cares to, why, I misdoubt the lady'd care to greet her friends again, nor live very long. What Mike can think of to do to a young lady, why, that's something that makes Turkey Nickerson feel like puking, and you can bet that there ain't much that does that to me."

"I am plowing my wits over, Doc, and I don't come up with nothing much to think of," Faro said.

"Nor I, my boy." The two men were moving across the flat land that led away from the deserted mining camp a good deal slower than they had approached it. Turkey Nickerson had increased his collection of Macduff bicycles by 200 percent, confiscating Doc's and

Faro's machines, and taken them to where Holly O'Devie's rented horse was tethered behind a ruined shed.

"You mount that, one behind the other," he had said. "It'll get you back to Durgin, you don't try to gallop it. And you'd best turn it in at the livery stable, so's there won't be any questions asked about it not coming back. 'Cause if there's questions asked, it could come to some being answered, and then folks coming out here wanting to talk to poor old Turkey Nickerson. And if that was to happen, why, there'd be things done to the young lady in there that'd make what Mike already done look like a Sunday school lesson."

Now, with his arms clasped around Doc's waist to keep his balance, Faro said, "Damn it, Doc, there's got to be something we can do that won't get Holly . . . that won't dip her into whatever kind of deep shit Nickerson's got in mind."

"Of course there is, my boy," Doc said. "But you don't know what it is, and I don't know what it is, so there might as well not be."

"Well, hell, Doc," Faro said, rocking back as Doc's bony shoulder, moving in time with the horse's jolting pace, connected briefly with his jawbone, "we got brains, ain't we? So let's use 'em on this."

"Ah, yes," Doc said. "You could cut cards with this Nickerson for Miss O'Devie's safety and contrive it so that you got the ace and him the jack. Or I could persuade him to trade her for half-shares in a bridge to be built across the Golden Gate, on which he would have a lifetime income from the tolls. I doubt, young Faro, that either of our stores of talents have much to offer for this predicament." He sighed. "As I thought back there, it would have simplified things considerably to have run him through some vital part with that cycle spoke when we had the chance."

"Hell, Doc, you don't just kill a man that's knocked out in cold blood," Faro said.

"The thing is, it would have been his blood that came into it, and not ours, and not Miss O'Devie's," Doc said. "How you get rid of someone like Turkey Nickerson doesn't seem to me to be all that important, so long as you can work out a way to do it."

"And right now, we ain't got a notion, is that it?"

Doc was silent for a moment, watching the shadow of the horse slide over the baked earth in front of them. Durgin was now visible as a few oblongs on the eastern horizon. "For a fact, we haven't," Doc said. "He's got her there, and he and his crew can see anyone coming, and he's crazy enough to do at least some of the things he said to her before anybody could get to him. Out of the question to go to the law or anything like that."

"Well, shit, Doc, do we just do like he says and give him the blueprints for how to take Polk Pilchard for his ox and his ass and everything that is his, the way it says in the Good Book?"

Doc shook his head. "No, we don't. Polk Pilchard's ass, and the rest of it, that's earmarked for us, my boy. We'll work out a way to grab it."

Returning the horse to the livery stable presented no problems; it was in an hour sooner than Holly O'Devie had contracted for, and the liveryman was glad enough of the unearned revenue not to question just who it was doing the returning.

"I don't think we want to share our fellow boarders' repast tonight, tasteful and sumptuous though it doubtless is," Doc said as he and Faro walked away from the stable.

"How come?"

"Miss O'Devie won't be there, and her absence from the table she normally graces with her presence will arouse comment. It will be recalled that she rented a horse this morning; it will then be found that the horse has been returned by Major Mordaunt and his new associate; and the major and his friend will be asked questions they won't care to answer. We're in for that, one way or another, in a while, but there's no point in getting the whole thing started up sooner than we have to. I recall I owe you some drinks at Callahan's over the race that brought us to that ill-omened place. Let's repair there, and study if the beneficent fluids may perhaps promote our powers of cerebration."

"Whatever you say, Doc. And besides that, I've found sometimes that having a drink or what helps you think a little clearer, too," Faro said.

Along with the drinks, Callahan was able to provide some red-hot chili for Doc and corned beef, cabbage and boiled potatoes for Faro, which went some little way toward soaking up the alcohol, but not very far. Faro was aware of feeling considerably fuzzy about the eyeballs and brain as the evening wore on, and he and Doc discussed what could be done about Holly O'Devie.

Doc belched and said, "A damn fool name for the stuff. Chilly's the one thing it isn't. Could about burn off the booze as if you'd set a match to it, the way it feels to me."

It seemed to Faro that this comment was not getting them any further along in going into Holly O'Devie's situation. "Thass as may be, Doc, though it ain't the same word, the food being named for one of them countries down aft of Mexico, I b'lieve, but the thing is, how do we get Holly away from that Turkey?"

"That's a country, too, but not in South America," Doc said, "so I don't see why you're bringing it up."

"Turkey Nickerson, Doc," Faro said.

"Ah. The thing to do about Turkey Nickerson is—the thing to do about Turkey Nickerson is," Doc said, then leaned forward, pillowing his head in his folded arms, and became silent.

Expect he's thinking it all out, Faro thought. Long-headed as he is, he'll come up with a plan, Doc will.

"Blake."

Faro looked up. Polk Pilchard was standing in front of him. "Running your bank tonight?"

"Ah. No. Taking a, like a holiday, see," Faro said.

"Care for some poker?"

"No. Another time."

Doc hoisted himself away from his arms and stared at Pilchard. "Ah, there, Polk Pilchard," he said.

"Been thinking about what you been telling me about that cycle race, Major," Pilchard said.

"Do that," Doc said cordially. "Think all you like. A man that doesn't think about what he's doing, why, that man's not a man, to my way of thinking. Think, that's Major Hilary Mordaunt's motto, and you'd be a better Pilchard for having it cross-stitched, framed and hung up over your desk, or any place you happen to be sitting with your eyes on the wall."

Pilchard blinked. "Well, since it don't seem that I'm to have any cards tonight, nor any talk about that cycle race, maybe I'd best get on home for once. Yeah, not a bad idea. Get me a bottle of rye from Callahan—and maybe some of what wine he's got, for the Mrs. I give her a taste or so of that, maybe she'll be a little more thawed out than what she is by custom."

As Pilchard moved off to the bar to discuss his prospective purchases with Callahan, Doc shook his head slightly. "Somewhere under the haze that's hanging about me," he said, "I sense that you and I may have struck the right chord with yonder Herring, young Faro. Forgot about that part of it, letting the mark see you don't give a damn. Next time he talks to either you or me, he'll be hot after what we're offering him, as he's seen that we're for the moment indifferent to it." He looked toward Pilchard and shook his head.

"Sober or drunk, I can't seem to see any way out of trying to find out what Nickerson says he wants to know, and telling it to him. I admit that Pilchard is a man who could be vastly improved by being robbed blind, but it goes against the grain to help someone else do it when you and I have that kind of idea in mind ourselves."

"Thing is," Faro said, "we know a little of what Turkey wants, like where the safe is, upstairs in the big bedroom, but not the rest of it, like when him and his boys could go in and get it without raising no ructions."

Doc shook his head. "And I doubt he'd settle for that alone, and then what he'd do to Miss Holly is something it'd take a lot more than the booze we've taken aboard here to forget about. So . . ."

"So maybe you or me or both of us has a talk with Pilchard tomorrow and finds out when he and Am—the Mrs. might chanst to be out or downstairs socializing or what, so's they wouldn't know that someone'd come in upstairs and was beggaring them," Faro said.

Doc reflected. "That seems to be the best scheme we can come up with at the moment, doesn't it?"

"I guess yeah, Doc."

"How does it strike you?"

"Shitty."

Another hour at Callahan's had not brought about any improvement in their plans, and toward midnight Faro and Doc made their way with some erratic footwork back to Mrs. Pyle's with the problem still unresolved in any satisfactory way.

Faro chuckled softly as they lurched along the darkened street. "This's hard going enough," he said, "but figger what it'd be like if we was both on cycles."

"Around in circles," Doc agreed. "Say, how come we're almost back to Callahan's?"

"Wrong turn some place," Faro said, and managed to point himself and Doc in the right direction.

A good deal longer after this exchange than he would have expected, Faro found himself in his room, dimly illuminated by a streetlight's rays coming in through the window. After wondering just how he had got there, and where Doc was—in the street? In his own room? Back at Callahan's?—he composed himself for a quiet night's repose by falling face-down on the bed and taking a mouthful of the pillowcase.

Skrtch. Tap.

Faro stirred. The noises that had awakened him were repeated, and he now realized that they were coming from the door. Someone was scratching at it, then giving it the lightest possible rap.

Doc, recovered a little from the evening's drinking and wanting a further, and soberer, conference? Faro realized that the booze fog had worn off in the main, leaving him mostly lightheaded, with a suggestion of a railroad spike driven into him somewhere above the temples.

He peered toward the window. The streetlamp was still the only source of illumination in that direction, so it had to be well before dawn, probably not much after two or so in the morning.

He rolled off the bed and padded in stockinged feet for the door—got my shoes off, if nothing else, he thought. Say, maybe Doc's come up with something real good—wouldn't be up himself if he hadn't, say nothing of inflicting cruel and unusual punishment by waking me up.

He opened the door and was for an instant firmly convinced that Callahan's bourbon had unexpected and dire ingredients in it, smooth though it tasted.

"Mr. Blake, I have to talk to you," Holly O'Devie said.

Chapter 12

Faro gaped at her.

"Mr. Blake," Holly O'Devie said again, "I've got to talk to you."

"And me to you, I'd guess," Faro said, collecting his faculties. "Come on in."

He fished a match from his trousers, found his way to the lantern on the table, lifted the chimney, struck the match, held it to the wick and lowered the chimney, wondering just what the hell had happened.

"Jesus," he said, "last I seed you, you was bound and gagged out there in Polk Pilchard's old mine, with Turkey Nickerson and them giving you a . . . well, a kind of bad time. 'S great to see you got away from 'em, and it's a relief to me in more ways 'n one, I can tell you. How in the name of the Almighty did you work that?"

Holly O'Devie, standing near the door, gazed at him

with wide eyes, then swayed. Faro stepped to her and held her upright. "Hell, after what you been through, you got a right to faint, you want to do that," he said.

"I . . . no, I just got a little dizzy for a minute," Holly O'Devie said. "But . . ."

"After that Mike . . . well, you don't want to think about that," Faro said. "But then . . . what happened? You manage to work them ropes loose from your wrists and then untie the rest of 'em around your ankles?"

"Uh," Holly O'Devie said faintly.

"And then I expect you found a way to sneak out of the mine and . . . Hey, you honest to God look like you're about to faint. You want a gollop of whiskey, just to get you out of the jangles?"

Holly O'Devie nodded, and Faro took his flask from his valise and poured a generous measure into the glass on his night stand and handed it to her.

She shuddered as she gulped it, then looked at him with widened eyes. "It was . . . I . . ."

"I can see it'd be hard for you to tell it, a thing like that," Faro said. He upended the flask into his mouth and took a swig. He had surely had enough with Doc at Callahan's, but that seemed to have worn off, and this sudden shock required a little lubrication to ease it. "So you snuck out when it was dark and . . . well, hell, you couldn't of walked it all that ways, not in the dark. What'd you do, take one of their horses and walk him away until you was so far off they wouldn't hear it when you set him at a trot?"

Holly O'Devie sipped the whiskey and nodded at him.

"I got to say," Faro said, "that is about the most sand I ever heared of in a woman, and no shame to a man neither. When I think about what them folks was fixing to do to you, it makes me come all over goose flesh—hell, sorry," he said, seeing that Holly O'Devie was visibly paling and swaying. "Sure thing, you don't want to have that recalled to you. But the major and I, we'd of worked out something to get you away, by this next sunset at the latest. Beats me what it would of been, but we'd of done it. Only now, it don't signify, as you're back here safe, and no Nickersons holding you hostage."

Holly O'Devie gave a mewing cry of distress and folded over onto Faro; he gripped her under the arms to hold her upright.

"Hey, it's all over now," he said. She gave a disconsolate wail—shit, it's getting to her now, and no wonder, Faro thought—and clutched him fiercely. What was it that that Mike was doing back there, anyhow? Something anybody'd want to forget, for sure.

"Oh," Holly O'Devie said. "You're . . . I'm glad you're here."

"Well, I'm glad you're here," Faro said. "A lot better than where you was this afternoon."

She shuddered against him. The tremor set up a response in him that he had not, considering the circumstances, been expecting, but there it was. Well, it wasn't all that long since they'd been humping like crazy, and maybe some more of the same was what she needed just now, a way to get rid of the stuff she'd been through.

Faro's hands roved Holly O'Devie's back, found a row of buttons and began working at them. She stiffened and pushed her hands against his chest.

"Now, hey," he said. "You've had a hard time today, and maybe the best thing's to find a way to forget about it. You and me, the other morning, that was some nice, wasn't it? Well, maybe that's the best medicine for what's troubling you right now, huh?"

"The other . . ."

"Bathroom, drying off, bedroom, remember?" Faro said.

"Oh . . . yes, that."

"Well, hey, if I figgered you wrong, lemme apologize," Faro said, feeling a touch of asperity.

"No . . . it's . . . oh . . ." Holly O'Devie slid her hands around to his back and clutched him hard once more, pressing herself against him. "Yes. Yes, I want that."

The dress peeled away from her under his fingers, then the camisole, drawers and stockings. Her body gleamed in the lamplight, tautly plump, like a ripe fruit, as he remembered her. His own clothes took longer to remove—there was enough of the discoordination remaining from the session at Callahan's to make unbuttoning his fly something approaching a nightmare—but he was soon next to her on the bed, holding her closely.

Holly O'Devie reached down to where his erection pressed against her belly and closed around it. "Yes," she said again and slid and arched until he was positioned to go into her.

The entrance was hard to find, but Faro moved until he had, and then thrust. It was slow going; Holly O'Devie was warm but dry, and he held himself back on the first thrust so as not to pain her. He stayed a moment before beginning the return motion and felt dampness enfolding him.

She moaned and moved against him. Her nipples grazed the tangle of hair on his chest, and her belly was slick under him. Her hands stroked his back, gently, with fingertips and palms, not digging with the nails, as she had before.

Holly's head lay sidewise on the pillow; her eyes were closed and her lips parted; she breathed in short gasps that matched the rhythm of his strokes.

Faro had the feeling that she was hardly aware of him, or at least of who he was. No matter; he was pleasuring her and himself, and that was what they both needed right now.

He slid a hand behind her buttocks and between, savoring how their firmness clenched and relaxed as she rose and fell in time with him. His forefinger probed, found what it sought; she gave a short whimper of negation, reached for his hand and moved it aside. Okay, not that this time, he thought.

It was quiet and simple, not adventurous and hectic as it had been that morning he'd dried her from her bath and taken her in here. And no wonder, Faro thought. I'm about half loaded still, and about half not woke up yet, and she's come through being kidnapped and whatever that Mike done, and getting out of there and back here. A wonder either of us is in shape to hump at all, but a damn good thing we can, as I doubt there's anything that'd do us more good just now.

He moved his hand to where her belly rubbed against his, then down, searching and parting her, feeling himself slide into and out of her, stroking and rubbing.

Holly O'Devie gave a sharp indrawn cry and arched strongly against him. He felt a sudden, soft constriction and a warm flooding around him, and then the quick, irreversible tide in his erection that sent him spasming inside her.

Faro was not sure how much later it was when he moved from where he lay sprawled on her and onto the rumpled sheet. She murmured sleepily as they turned and found comfortable positions, and wound up nested like spoons in a drawer, her back to his front. Just before sleep claimed him, he thought he heard her murmur, "Junie . . ."

Well, hell. Not the first time I been with a woman

who had another man on her mind. Junius who, I wonder?

When he came awake, not far after sunrise, she was gone.

Faro had meant to talk to Doc in his room before breakfast, but had relapsed into sleep and barely managed to make the tag end of breakfast. He found Doc at the table as Mrs. Pyle took away empty plates and fetched him his own repast. Faro refused the oatmeal, but tucked into the bacon, eggs and fried potatoes with a relish that surprised him. Fellows that have an appetite problem ought to try what I was at in the small hours, he thought. Try it in the hospitals and you'd have a waiting list of customers.

Doc eyed him gloomily. "Advancing age must be getting to me. All I could manage was coffee and toast."

"Not enough to keep a bird alive, Major," Mrs. Pyle said. "There, now, Mr. Blake, you've got what you need to keep you going, and I'll be at my dishes."

When the landlady had left, Faro grinned at Doc and said, "Surprised not to see Holly here. She's pretty set on having her meals regular and copious."

"Well, damn it," Doc said, "naturally she's . . ." He stopped and studied Faro carefully. "It's not Faro Blake's way, as Master Nickerson would put it, to dither. I divine that you are working your way around to tell me something of more than ordinary interest."

Faro told him something—but by no means all—of Holly O'Devie's late-night visit. "She, uh, wasn't making too much sense, and she didn't go into no details, but the main thing is that she's got away from that Nickerson and his crowd."

"So it is," Doc said thoughtfully. "We can draw out a full narration when it seems appropriate. And we can also now stop racking our brains for ways to accommodate Nickerson. He's got no hold on us anymore."

"Hey, right," Faro said, cheered to realize that Turkey Nickerson and his needs were no longer a problem. He sipped at his coffee and grimaced, then felt in his coat pocket for his flask. "Want some, Doc?" he asked as he poured a dollop into his cup. "Makes it drinkable."

"After last night?" Doc looked at him sourly. "A drink in the morning to cure a hangover's the sure way to ruin and degradation, young Faro, no matter how damned good it might taste. . . . Yes, a generous splash, if you don't mind."

Braced by the fortified coffee, Doc began to consider with enthusiasm his plans for the day. "Been turning over in my mind how to get Pilchard ready for the gaff, and I've come up with a notion. You gave it to me, in fact, yesterday, with your idle talk about a posse taking out after Nickerson—can the faithful horse outrun an expert cyclist on level ground?"

"Would think it could," Faro said.

"Perhaps. But, win or lose, such a contest would arouse interest in the machines hereabouts, and that's bound to work to our benefit. Polk Pilchard will become inflamed with the desire to gain the renown he craves among the Durginites. It should be no great matter to arrange an impromptu race. A little talk about the noon hour at Callahan's, a veiled sneer at the quality of the local horseflesh as compared to what I'm used to in Her Majesty's armies, and the thing's set up."

"On one side, it is, maybe," Faro said. "But for a race, you got to have two parties. Whereat is this expert cyclist you was talking of?"

Doc smiled broadly. "Sitting across the table from me right now. After all, you beat me yesterday, didn't you? Victory has its costs, young Faro, as well as defeat."

Faro stared glassily at the surging hindquarters and pounding legs of the horse in front of him. Praise the Almighty, Doc and that Barnet settled on half a mile for the damn thing, he thought—keeping up this pace, I couldn't last a yard longer. But, damn, I ain't all that far behind that horse's ass at that. His legs pistoned on the pedals, driving him and the bicycle forward at a dizzying pace. Doc, consulting the manual, had spent much of the morning adjusting the machine for best performance, tightening a nut here and loosening a bearing there. His substitution of an optional larger rear gearwheel would, he claimed, come close to doubling the vehicle's speed—"Provided, of course, that you can get it moving fast in the first place, but that's up to you, my boy."

All the same, the horse was drawing slowly but steadily ahead as they approached the finish line outside of town. Faro redoubled his effort, wondering why—it wasn't his way to get into something where he had to work to win. Then the horse was suddenly larger in his vision, rearing up and turning sideways. A flash of white went across the roadway from right to left and disappeared into the sparse sagebrush. Faro leaned to the left and sent the speeding cycle past the horse, which had not yet regained its forward motion, and streaked toward the crowd at the finish line, rolling past them until the machine slowed of its own accord and he was able to place a trembling foot on the ground.

"A unique demonstration," Doc called to the crowd. "While the valiant equine may have a marginally better turn of speed, it is subject to alarms, such as the passing jack rabbit, which negate that advantage. Does the bicycle shy at a jack rabbit, or any other such distraction of the countryside? The question answers itself—no! And, ladies and gentlemen, consider the matter of feed and stabling. The cycle merely requires a squirt of oil now and then, and a tarpaulin to keep the dews of night from causing rust. And, of course, there is nothing to clean up."

Faro listened to him go on in this vein for some time. When he finished and came over to him, Faro said, "Hey, I won that, didn't I?"

"So you did, my boy."

"I bet, give me some more practice on the fucker, I could of done it even without that jack rabbit bolting acrost the road."

"Possibly," Doc said.

"Damn, I am tuckered out enough to lie down right here with a case of the heaves. But it feels pretty good to of done that hard work and come out good at the end of it. Lucky thing about the rabbit, there."

Doc looked at him. "If you're going to work much more with Jackson Lafitte Prentiss, or Major Hilary Mordaunt, or any other of my avatars, young Faro, you'd best stop thinking that luck comes into it. A silver dollar to a farm lad and the agile rodent was in place to perform his part. Now," Doc went on, "the main damn thing is that Polk Pilchard wasn't around to see it, which discounts the benefit of the whole enterprise by about half. All the same, he'll hear of it in due course, so the chief point will be made."

"Well, shit, Doc," Faro said, still feeling the giddiness of his arrowing through the noontime air, "what I feel is, that's the first time I was ever in a race, and I knowed I didn't have no chance to win, and I won the sumbitch. And I am feeling pretty good about that, jack rabbits or no. Less go on down to Callahan's and celebrate up on that."

"We got blind drunk at Callahan's last night and came up pretty wavery this morning," Doc said.

"Right," Faro said. "And look where it got us. You think I'd of won the race, or come close to it, but for that? Some stuff in the world, Doc, you got to do with half a load on."

Doc studied him carefully for a moment. "There may be something in what you say. In any case, the heat of the day and your honorable exertions would seem to require liquid restoratives. Perhaps it will inspire us to perfect our plans for relieving Polk Pilchard of what we can. The timing's something to consider there, my boy. Your poker game first, then the race . . . no, by George, have them both at the same time! The race'll be an added draw for the sports, cinch it that they'll be willing to come on here—the first bicycle race in Arizona Territory! Oh, yes, Polk Pilchard'll lap that up. Let's get on to Callahan's and work it out. Pilchard'll surely be there, and we'll put it to him on the spot."

By late evening, Pilchard had not made his customary appearance at Callahan's, and Doc and Faro had bettered their state of the previous evening, both of them having been bought drinks by Durginites in appreciation of the afternoon's entertainment.

"Pilchard ought to be here," Doc said, looking around the saloon.

"Well, he ain't," Faro said.

"Can you be sure?"

"Pretty much. There ain't but maybe five or six fellows here now, near as I can count, and there ain't none of them a Polk Pilchard."

"He could be in disguise," Doc said, wagging one finger at Faro.

"Why?"

Doc shrugged. "If a man understood all the ins and outs of Polk Pilchard's mind, likely he'd be in danger of turning into Polk Pilchard himself, and that'd be a lousy way to be, wouldn't it?"

"For sure," Faro said, considering the thought. "Say, Major, d'you think it'd be worse to be Polk Pilchard or Turkey Nickerson?"

Doc stared glassily at the table. "Not that much to choose between them as people, I'd say. Nickerson's plain crazy, of course, but that's not a bad way to be if you've got to be him. And Pilchard is mean and stupid, but on the other hand he's got a lot of money and a damned good-looking woman for his wife, but on the third hand he's made so that he doesn't get much enjoyment out of either of 'em. So I'd say it's a tossup."

"Thing about Polk Pilchard, you can't count on him," Faro said. "Night after night after night after night, he's here at Callahan's looking for a game or what, and now when we want him particular, he ain't."

"When you can't depend on a mark to show up to be taken, what's the world coming to?" Doc said.

"Well, by God, if he don't come to us, we can go to him, like that fellow and the mountain you tole me of once," Faro said firmly. "Less you and me, Doc, less you and me go on over to his place and put it to him, get him to say if he's going to do my game and your race, tell him it's time to fish or get off the pot."

"And if he doesn't like it, he can go piss up a rope," Doc said.

"Or on Turkey Nickerson, for all of me," Faro said.

The recollection of their deft exchange of wit sustained them in high good humor during their reeling journey to Polk Pilchard's house.

Faro banged on the knocker several times. "Don't hear nobody coming," he said after a while.

"Somebody's home," Doc said, looking up at the parlor window, which sent a pale wash of light into the dark.

"Maybe the firedamp got 'em," Faro said vaguely. He beat another tattoo on the door, with the same lack of result.

"Maybe he or the Mrs., or both, are out back in the kitchen having a snack," Doc said. "Folks can get peckish, this hour of the evening."

"With Polk Pilchard, it ain't peckerish, anyways, what I hear," Faro said. "Okay, less go 'round back and knock on the door there."

They moved away from Pilchard's front steps and around to the side of the massive house, feeling their way among the spiky ornamental shrubbery that lined it. "Man must pay an almighty water bill to keep this stuff growing," Faro said.

"I believe I'm in a position to help him out," Doc said, pausing beside a bush and fumbling at the front of his trousers.

"Me too." After treating Pilchard's shrubbery to rather more than a quart of Callahan's liquor, as altered by its passage through their bodies, Doc and Faro made a stab at rebuttoning their trousers, then lurched on toward the rear of the house.

Faro was suddenly aware of a moving form in the darkness, of a chunky sound, like a maul hitting a piece of wood—and then of a sharp pain in his head and the earth coming up to meet him. His last dim thought was that it was awfully early for a hangover to catch up with him.

Chapter 13

When Faro awoke, it was to find Turkey Nickerson standing over him and glaring at him. As at their last interview, he was bound, with coils of rope securing his wrists and ankles. He turned his head and saw Doc, blinking in the light from the lantern on the table, also trussed up and lying beside him.

It was the same chamber in the abandoned mine, the same circumstances and the same Turkey Nickerson. And why the hell would that be? Faro wondered.

"Now I can't understand you fellows, so I can't," Turkey Nickerson said.

"The incomprehension is mutual," Doc said. "I can't think why we're here once more. Surely—"

"It was a shock to me, a real shock," Nickerson said, "that you fellows didn't show up here at sundown. A man that's given an undertaking and don't keep it, why, that's beyond the range of Turkey Nickerson's wits, so it is. Plus which it shakes me to think you'd leave that sweet young lady to what Mike'd do to her. A man would have to have a heart of stone to do a thing like that."

Faro opened his mouth to speak, then shut it. Turkey Nickerson was about as slovenly a bandit as he had ever come across, but it hardly seemed credible that he would have been unaware of the escape of his hostage. Maybe Mike had decided it would be better to keep Holly O'Devie's absence quiet for a while, out of a desire to avoid the effects of Turkey Nickerson's volatile temper. In any case, there didn't seem any point just now in telling what he knew. There might come a time when tossing the news at Nickerson might put him off balance, to Faro's and Doc's advantage.

He glanced sidewise at Doc and caught the sudden narrowing of the old man's eyes, which he took as a signal that Doc had had the same thought.

"It was all set up just right and neat," Nickerson said, "all worked out just the way I'd planned it. And then you fellows spoiled it by not showing up. I'll never, if I live to be forty-one, figure out why you done me that way."

He looked at them broodingly. "The trouble you've put me to'd make a strong man weep, so it would. Me and Ben, we had to ride into town in the dark, once you two didn't show up, so as to see what might be going on. All the way in, was hoping to come acrost you, with some excuse for why you was late and anxious to make up for it by giving me all you'd learned. But no, wasn't nobody on the road, bar a farmer that we took his money off of, knocked him on the head and left him in his cart to be took wherever his mule has a mind to go."

Nickerson pulled out a revolver and laid it on the table next to the lantern. "In fairness all 'round, I ought to corpse you on the spot for the aggravation," he said. "But it ain't Turkey Nickerson's way to act hasty. It appears to me you fellows might still have some information I could use, so I'd best find it out beforehand."

"Ah . . ." Doc said. "How does it come about that you happened to be where Mr. Blake and I were?"

Right, Doc, Faro thought. Keep the fucker talking and we've bought ourselves some time at least.

"When you fellows let me down so bad, seemed best to have myself a look at Polk Pilchard's place, at least from the outside, so's we'd have a notion of where the windows and doors was, the view of it the houses on the same street had, so's we could do the business quick and neat when the time come for it. So we was along there, and then along come you fellows, banging away at the front door like musketry."

Nickerson glared at them and spun the cylinder of the revolver, squinting at it as if checking to make sure it was fully loaded. "When you went around the side of the house, Ben and me, we decked you, and throwed you over our horses and come out here. Seemed the best way to make sure we could have ourselfs a talk, and see what was to be done about how you broke faith with me. If I suspicioned that you was going there to warn Polk Pilchard about what I had in mind, I believe I'd loose this off at you until it was empty, and so would you be in a while. Of your blood's what I mean," he explained, stretching his lips in a grin.

"We were calling on Mr. Pilchard on another matter entirely," Doc said hastily. "To do with promoting the fortunes of the Macduff and Sons Bicycle Company, and nothing in our minds about your own enterprise."

"That's as may be," Nickerson said. "But it don't set well with me, what you done. Lemme see. Should I have Mike bring the young lady out and do the kind of things he likes with her, so's you can kind of have a sample of what's in store for her, and maybe change your minds about throwing in with me, sincere and wholehearted?"

"I assure you that it would not affect us," Doc said. "Miss O'Devie, while an estimable young woman, is not a major concern to Mr. Blake and myself. The reason for our failure to keep the rendezvous was simply that you had no leverage. We would regret it if your Mike performed a variety of unspeakable acts on her, culminating in some abomination that resulted in her painful death, but it would not alter our resolve to have nothing to do with your plans." Doc spoke, Faro knew, with the confidence imparted by the knowledge that Holly O'Devie was nowhere around for this program to be put into effect.

"You ever come acrost Mike before?" Turkey Nickerson asked. "That's just about the way he likes to operate, for sure. Well, well, then, maybe it's come to corpsing time, for if I don't have no handle on you, that may be the best thing. If a man ain't to be trusted, there's just no further use for him, that's Turkey Nickerson's way of thinking."

"On the other hand," Doc said quickly, eyeing Nickerson's hand as it reached for the revolver, "it's possible that something could be—"

A shout and a scuffling sound came from behind Turkey Nickerson. His hand darted for the gun, and he turned to face the source of the noise. "Mike—in here!" he called.

The man Faro and Doc had seen hustling the bound Holly O'Devie into and out of the chamber the day before appeared, carrying a Colt's. Another man, a stranger to them, entered from the corridor leading to the mine entrance, frog-marching a man in front of him, with a pistol held to his head.

The captive stared wildly around the room, taking in

the presence of Faro and Doc, and the revolver in Turkey Nickerson's hand.

"Gimme that gun!" Polk Pilchard squealed. "I want first shot at that gambler!"

"Why?" Turkey Nickerson asked, echoing Faro's unspoken question.

"Despoiler of my home, that's why!" Pilchard said. "Came into my house as a guest, then came back and despoiled my wife in the upstairs bedroom. I want to put a slug in his balls so he dies screaming."

To Faro's dismay, Turkey Nickerson seemed to be considering this proposition seriously. "Dear me," Doc murmured softly, "I do wish that you could keep your amorous propensities from interfering with business, my boy. It's not the act itself, but the indiscretion, that creates problems."

"And after that, I want to put a couple holes in Major Mordaunt, there, another despoiler," Polk Pilchard said.

"Oh, Doc," Faro murmured reproachfully.

"Hell," Doc muttered, "if he's so dead set against despoilers, he'd have to do away with about half the male population of Durgin, from what I understand."

"Well, now, Mr. Polk Pilchard," Nickerson said, "why don't you just sit—no, I'm sitting and there's only the one chair—why don't you just lean over against the wall there, comfortable as you can get, and tell me all about this? Not armed, is he, Ben?"

Ben flourished a shotgun. "Had this on him. Took it. Nothing else."

Nickerson nodded. "Good. Now, Mr. Pilchard, you just account to me how it comes you're here."

Pilchard glared venomously at Doc and Faro. "Meant to talk to them two last night at Callahan's, but they was orry-eyed and in no state of mind for it, not talk nor a game or so, so's a man could keep in form. So I got me a bottle for some home drinking, and some sweet wine, the kind that my wife likes, for her. She's a cold fish mostly, but sometimes when she's taken a little aboard she's willing to . . . well, be more of a wife to me, like, the way I like it." Faro briefly wondered what needs Pilchard had that Amelia Pilchard's normal performance would not satisfy, and decided he wouldn't want to know.

"So I had me some drinks, and 'Melia, she had her some drinks, and we got to . . . or close to . . . anyhow, she took a fit of some kind, and wouldn't have it, and she come out all in a rush about how this Blake and the major was more man than me, and when they was there, and so on. So I hit up on her some, and drank off the rest of the bottle that night, and stayed in bed all today, getting myself set for going after these two. And then, come midnight or about, I heard a banging at the front door, and there was Blake and the major, come right to me."

"Wisht I'd been so lucky," Turkey Nickerson said.

"So I went down and got me down my shotgun and loaded it, and went to the front door. But they wasn't there no more, and then I heard hoofbeats going down the street, and figured it was them, riding off. So I went out back and saddled up and came out this way. Couldn't follow trail much in the dark, but I come across some horseshit that felt fresh, so it seemed to me they might have come on to here, and I came for a look, and your man, he jumped me and took my gun. And as you don't seem to be friends of theirs, I'd appreciate to have it back, or the lend of yours, so's I can give them what they deserve."

"Interesting idea," Turkey Nickerson said. "Well, you want something from me, and I want something from you, so maybe we can work out a deal."

"What d'you want from me?" Pilchard asked suspiciously.

"Everything," Turkey Nickerson said.

"What?"

"Well, no. Not your furniture, nor your house deed, nor the clothes you stand up in," Nickerson amended. "The money you've got around your place'll do me and the boys fine. If you can work it to take a man's last cent, that should be enough, why be greedy?—that's Turkey Nickerson's motto."

"Well . . ." Pilchard blinked and looked around the rough-hewn rocky chamber, at the grinning Nickerson, at Ben and Mike, and at the bound figures of Doc and Faro. He seemed to come out of the fever of outrage that had possessed him and to become aware of just what kind of situation he was in.

"There's . . . I don't keep much cash in the house," he said.

"Then you won't mind letting us have a look at what there is," Nickerson said.

"I . . . listen, you can't make me show you—"

"Ever had a .38 slug through your kneecap?" Nickerson said carelessly.

"Uh . . . no."

"We live and learn, like the saying is," Nickerson said. He rose from his chair and stepped backward toward the corridor leading to the mine entrance, then raised the revolver. "Don't like to shoot sitting," he said. "Standing up, a little distance to make the thing interesting, that's Turkey Nickerson's way."

"Hey, now," Pilchard said, "listen, I'll tell you, show you—"

Nickerson raised the revolver. "Sure you will. 'Cause you won't want to lose the other kneecap. I'll do the first one just to show you I'm serious, then we can have ourselfs a talk."

Ben and Mike were staring at Pilchard with interest, presumably waiting to see what his knee would look like when Nickerson's bullet smashed it—out here, Faro supposed, fun was hard to come by—and Nickerson's attention was fixed on his victim. Doc and Faro were concentrating on Nickerson, both of them trying desperately to figure out how they were going to come out of this with whole skins.

Their eyes bulged as they saw movement in the dimness behind Turkey Nickerson, then a swift chopping motion of a revolver butt slamming against the bandit's head.

Nickerson fell forward in a heap on the floor. Ben and Mike stood frozen for an instant, then Ben started to raise the revolver that had been dangling negligently by his side.

Holly O'Devie shot him in the arm and he reeled against the wall, yelping and dropping his weapon.

Mike backed up, staring like a spooked horse.

"Where did you—" "Hey, how did you—" Faro and Doc said in unison. Mike gave a low horrified wail, as if he had seen a ghost. Polk Pilchard said nothing, but sagged into the wall, flexing his knee as if to reassure himself he still had the use of it.

Holly O'Devie gestured with the barrel of her gun, from which a wisp of smoke still trailed. "Get her," she said.

Mike continued to goggle. "Wherever she is, go get her," Holly O'Devie said. "By when I say three or I'll kill you now. One."

"But," Mike said, "you're—"

"Two."

Mike turned and scuttled from the chamber. "Hey," Faro said, "why'd you send him off, and for who? That jasper could run off and no one the wiser."

"He won't," Holly O'Devie said. "There's nothing in

that direction but two dead-end shafts. The only way out is through here."

"How'd you . . ."

Faro stopped in shock as, contrary to his predictions, Mike reappeared around the rocky corner.

With him, bound and gagged, was Holly O'Devie.

Chapter 14

"Well, of course there's no such person as Holly O'Devie," Holly O'Devie said. She pointed at her draggled double, who had just been released from her bonds. "That's Juniper Ginn, and I'm Geneva, we're twins."

"Providing a double portion of beauty in a weary world," Doc said gallantly.

A comatose Turkey Nickerson and a respectful Ben and Mike were being tied up by Faro and Doc. "That one," Juniper said, "Mike. Tie him tight as you can, snug the ropes till they won't go any further."

"It'd cut off his circulation, and his hands and feet would get gangrene," Doc said. "Amputation would be an almost inevitable consequence."

"Most of him would be better amputated," Juniper said. Faro, remembering that she had spent more than a day in Mike's custody, could not find fault with the judgment. She stared briefly at Pilchard, gave a slight start as if something had occurred to her and slipped out of the chamber. Probably got took sudden with the need to empty her waterworks, Faro thought, and went down a ways for a place she could use. Don't expect that Mike give her much chance to ease herself while she was tied up.

"Gimme that gun, woman," Polk Pilchard said. "I got me a couple of home despoilers to ventilate." He moved toward Geneva, then stopped as she leveled the revolver at him.

"Polk Pilchard," she said, "I'd stand anyone a drink that despoiled your home, or brought your gray hairs in sorrow to the gravel and defiled it afterwards."

"Hey," Polk Pilchard said, "what'd I ever do to you?"

"Nothing," Geneva Ginn said. "But our uncle, Norris McTeague, you certainly did something to him, unloading this worthless mine on him, after you and him had been partners for years."

"Aha!" Doc said, finishing trussing Mike, though not as rigorously as Juniper had requested. "Then . . . yes. You two were the heirs our fowl player here"—he gestured at Turkey Nickerson—"robbed, then burned out."

"We were and are," Geneva Ginn said. "Junie and I, we knew Uncle Norris was rich, or thought we knew it, but when he died, we found there wasn't much money. The house and furniture were worth a lot, though, so we didn't care much about that. In spring, we went down to San Francisco to see what there was in the shops and the theaters, and take some time to figure out what we'd do—sell the house and stuff for what we could get, was what it came out to, and that would do us nicely."

She looked longingly at Turkey Nickerson over the sight on the revolver she held. "But when we came back, the place had burned. Well, that wasn't too bad, 'cause Uncle Norris had had it insured right up to the rafters, and it meant about as much money as we'd have got by selling everything, maybe more."

"A good outcome for you," Doc said.

"Too good," Juniper Ginn said, returning to the chamber. "The police and the insurance folks looked it over, and it was clear that the fire'd been set. And there wasn't any reason for it, since we didn't have any enemies, so . . ."

"Even though Junie and I were away in San Francisco, everybody thought we'd hired it done," Geneva Ginn said. "For the insurance money, d'you see?"

"A device not unknown to some merchants of my acquaintance during periods of financial upset," Doc said. "But here, the imputation was clearly unjust, the arson being an act of spite on the part of Nickerson, here."

"Well, we knew we hadn't done it," Juniper Ginn said, approaching the table and contriving to step into Mike's midsection as he lay bound on the floor. Mike convulsed and pushed an agonized squeal through his gag; Juniper smiled with satisfaction.

"But we didn't know who had," Geneva Ginn said. "And the police and the insurance people were talking to each other, and the insurance wasn't being paid off. And we got word through a friend in the police department that there was talk of getting out a warrant for our arrest."

"So you fled, a natural precaution," Doc said. "But why here?"

"Well, there was one thing," Juniper Ginn said slowly. "The Good Indian deed."

"Uncle Norris had it framed and hanging on the wall in his library," Geneva Ginn said.

"Because it reminded him, he said, never to work

with a partner again or to trust anybody much in the way of business." Juniper gave Polk Pilchard a cold look.

"And it happened that a couple of walls of the library were all that was left standing of the house," Geneva said. "And Junie and I, we noticed the bare hook and the sort of lighter square spot where the deed had been, and we could see that it hadn't fallen down into the mess and such underneath, so it seemed to us that somebody had to have taken it. And that somebody had to be the one that set the fire."

"Why anybody'd have wanted it was more than we could figure just then—though I can see it now," Juniper said, drawing a surprised glance from her twin. "But anyhow, it was the only clue we had, that somebody'd taken the Good Indian deed. And we figured, if he wanted that, maybe he'd come along here to have a look at it."

"So we got ourselves tickets to Durgin," Geneva said. "And on the way, we worked it out that we didn't have all that much money to live on while we were finding out if we could catch hold of the man that set the fire and get him arrested, so we wouldn't be arrested ourselves and get the insurance money, too."

"So, being twins, well . . . I rented the room from Mrs. Pyle, and Gen came in the back way when nobody was looking, and we took turns at meals and such, so's it seemed there was only one of us, and so only one board to pay."

Faro had deduced this revelation a little in advance of its actual disclosure and was busily trying to work out which Holly—Geneva or Juniper—he had encountered when. No wonder "Holly" had such an appetite at meals—she had been eating for two, in a manner of speaking, with only one or two appearances a day possible at the table.

And no wonder she—they—had been discernibly different in bed.

"We tried to be careful," Juniper said, "but we . . . almost got caught, sometimes." She gave Faro a quick smile. Yes, she'd be the one that'd been in the bathtub the second time, and then the drying off and the quick trot down to his room. . . . Then she'd have no way of knowing about the session with Geneva last night, not until the two girls had had a chance to talk. He wondered what their feelings would be about having shared the same man, without him knowing it.

"And it seemed to us," Geneva said, "that, there being two of us when everybody thought there was only one, it might be that if we had to do something out of the way to find out what we wanted to know, it'd make things easier. Like if one of us was accused of something against the law, it'd help if it could be proved that one of us was somewhere else at the time—the witnesses would be confused."

"An admirable arrangement should you consider a life of crime," Doc said. "Though I think the chief result has been to confuse Mr. Blake and myself concerning your—no, your sister's—presence or absence in this desolate spot. I shudder to think what the consequences might have been if we had gone on much longer under the fictitious assurance that you had escaped."

Juniper moved away from the table and stepped down hard; something between a sob and a whine erupted through Mike's gag. "Ah," Doc said. "It's . . . there's a kind of tradition about not abusing helpless prisoners."

"Fine," Juniper said. "I'll keep to it, scrupulous as you please. After I've caught up."

"And after we'd been here about a week, we decided

we weren't getting anywhere, just poking around town," Geneva said. "So yesterday, we worked it out that Junie would ride out here and see if there was any sign that anybody'd been around the Good Indian."

"And I came out, and the three of them jumped me," Juniper said. "And they tied me up and shoved me back at the end of the shaft, where the diggings finished, and . . ." She cast a glance at Pilchard that seemed to reflect amusement and secret knowledge. "Anyway, then the major and Mr. Blake came in and got caught as well, and Nickerson made them promise to help him rob Polk Pilchard—"

"We agreed only to keep him from, ah, further outrages on your person," Doc said quickly, noting Pilchard's grimace of rage.

Juniper shrugged. "Well, when you didn't turn up when you were supposed to, it looked like it would be really hard going with me for a while. But then Nickerson and Ben rode off, leaving Mike with orders not to damage me—much—until Nickerson had worked out what was going on. And then . . . well, you know the rest of it, I guess."

Faro thought briefly. "Well, I guess that about takes care of it all. Nickerson's got the deed, which the only place he could of got it from is the house he burned, and there's the major and me to tell that we heard him boast of it, if it comes to that. So you're off the hook for the burning of your place and shouldn't have no trouble about the insurance no more. And this crowd"—he gestured at Ben, Mike and the now wakeful Nickerson —"has got some time to do on account of what they done here, let alone Turkey's stretch in the Idaho pen that he ain't finished and whatever else them two might be wanted for. So—"

"Ladies," Polk Pilchard said plaintively, "you may

think I done your uncle wrong, but that's along of your not understanding the way of business. But it'd be real nice of you to let me kill these fellows."

"Why?" Geneva, like Turkey Nickerson before her, asked.

"They are home despoilers," Polk Pilchard said. "The old man, he despoiled my wife three, four times, best she can remember, and the young one but the once, though she said it was despoiling enough to count for half a dozen."

"Congratulations, my boy," Doc whispered.

"Huh," Geneva Ginn said, casting an interested glance at Faro. Then her eyes swiveled toward her twin, catching her at giving him a similar look, blending appraisal and recollection. Both girls' faces tightened a little, then relaxed. Guess twins don't need to send each other telegrams to know what's been going on, Faro thought.

"We're not interested in your domestic problems, Mr. Pilchard," Geneva said. "If your wife finds it necessary to seek her pleasures aside from what you provide, I'd say she's sensible . . . and lucky if she finds what she's after."

"You can't go up against Polk Pilchard," the ex-mineowner said. "I'll—"

"You won't do very much, Mr. Pilchard," Juniper Ginn said. "Not against the legal owners of the Good Indian mine, that's going to be the biggest thing in Durgin once again."

"What?" "What?" "What?" "What?" Doc, Faro, Geneva and Pilchard spoke as if in well-rehearsed unison.

Juniper looked at all four of them. "I told you they kept me at the end of the shaft. Well, I was all tied up, and the only thing I could think of was to try to find a way to get the ropes off my hands so I could untie the rest and maybe escape. So I inched up against the rocks in back and rubbed the ropes against them. And some of the rocks came away, but the ropes didn't fray, far as I could see. And I rubbed against the rocks that were exposed, but it didn't seem to do any good, as if they were soft.''

"What's that got to do with—" Polk Pilchard started to say.

"I didn't notice till the ropes were cut off me and I took a look at them, a few minutes back," Juniper Ginn said. "But . . . take a look yourself." She held up a handful of cut ropes. They were the pale tan of hemp . . . except where streaks of bright yellow ran along them.

"Lemme see!" Polk Pilchard said, grabbing the ropes. He scraped a fingernail on one yellow streak. "Gold!" he said. "Soft's butter, about, the pure stuff!"

Juniper Ginn nodded. "That's why it didn't do anything to the ropes. You must have stopped digging just before the biggest lode of all—and thought you were being clever by selling Uncle Norris your half-interest in a worthless mine. A dozen years, a little water trickling down, freezing in winter, cracking the rock away, and there's a vein showing that a child could go into and dig out with a spoon." She took the lantern from the table. "Let's all go back and have a look at the rock, to make sure of it. But I haven't any doubt. Oh, Mr. Polk Pilchard, we're going to be richer than you ever dreamed of, with all your cheating! And you could have had a half-share in it, if you'd been honest!"

Chapter 15

"I don't know that I've ever seen a stranger caravan than this, or anything near it," Doc observed.

Faro, surveying the procession making its way toward Durgin along the level road, had to agree. The setting full moon picked them out and cast shadows toward their destination: Juniper Ginn mounted behind Geneva on Turkey Nickerson's horse; Polk Pilchard on his own mount, leading Ben's and Mike's animals, the first of which bore the trussed form of Nickerson, with his slighter assistants slung across the back of the second; Doc and himself wobbling ahead on their retrieved bicycles, with Doc holding onto the machine Nickerson had escaped from the workshop on and wheeling it along.

"What're we going to do with Turkey and them, we get back to town?" Faro asked.

"Stuff him with Ben and Mike, and roast him, that'd be the sensible thing," Doc said. "But I expect there are some laws against that. No, I think we'll have to find some policeman or other and turn them over, along with enough testimony from all of us to keep them mewed up for a while."

Polk Pilchard's voice drifted over to them from where he rode next to the twins. "Now that deed, I don't know but what it ain't flawed some, I used a cheap kind of a lawyer when it was drawn up. If I was to look into it and it wouldn't hold up, why, I'd be willing to do the straight thing and pay you ladies back what poor McTeague paid me for my half-share. Plus interest at the going rate for a dozen years, as'd be only fair dealings."

"Mr. Pilchard," Juniper Ginn said, "we wouldn't think of going back into partnership with you. Meaning no disrespect, it just seems better to Gen and me to see to our own interests. If we have to, we'll settle in Durgin and run the Good Indian."

"If you have to . . . Well, ladies, though it's got some fine folks, I'd have to admit that Durgin's not the kind of garden spot they say Californy is. A brace of young women that had a good sum of money in hand, why, they could live out there and never have to worry about such things as how much to cut miners' wages, or how much to pay out to widows when there's a cave-in."

"There's a thought there, Mr. Pilchard," Juniper Ginn said.

"We could maybe talk about it at lunch at your boardinghouse," Polk Pilchard said. "Ma Pyle takes in casuals at meals for not much."

"The Butler House, I'd say," Juniper Ginn said. "We've never been able to afford to eat there, and if it turns out that we're not to stay on here, I'd like to try it."

"The Butler House it is," Pilchard said.

"They going to let that Pilchard eel them out of owning a gold mine that's going to pay out as big's it looks to be?" Faro asked Doc.

Though the moonlight was pale, he could see the sidewise shake of Doc's head. "It has the sound of it," Doc said. "But I don't see those young ladies as marks. If Pilchard takes them for such, he could be in for a surprise."

Once again there was no Holly O'Devie at Mrs. Pyle's breakfast table. Faro supposed that both girls were sleeping in their room, fatigued from their exertions of the night before and confident of a good feed at noontime in any case. He doubted that they would let Polk Pilchard handle the ordering of their lunches.

Turkey Nickerson and his henchmen had been delivered to a sleepy constable and locked up in the early hours of the morning, and Faro and Doc had got to bed not much after four. The sliced steak and eggs that Mrs. Pyle was providing this morning went some way toward revivifying Faro, and seemed to be having the same effect on Doc.

"We're going to have to testify against that trio, my boy," Doc said as they met for a conference in his room after breakfast. "Get up in court and have lawyers asking things about us."

"Not if we ain't here, Doc," Faro said. "There is trains in a couple directions, four, five times a day."

"But if we cut out, then the whole business with Pilchard is done with," Doc said.

Faro sighed. "What with all that was going on last night, you might of lost sight of the fact that Pilchard is carrying on some about us being despoilers. I would say that the big cycle race and the big poker game are just about scratched at the post by now."

Doc sighed. "You may be right. But I still feel that there's got to be a way to take Pilchard for a good round sum, if only I could work it out, despoilings or no."

"Well, I wouldn't mind having that class of fellows come into my place, sure and I wouldn't," Callahan said. "Be something of a draw, so it would."

"And there'd be others, tourists, you might say, that'd be drawn by the races," Barnet said. "Some'd be bound to come into my store as customers, and I could start up a temporary sideline in hokey-pokey wagons and other such, to take care of 'em while they're here. Yes, it'd be good for business."

"Well, then," Doc said, pursuing the scheme he and Faro had arrived at in his room, "we'll take it that you'll put in a good word for these harmless yet diverting enterprises with Mr. Polk Pilchard. It's one thing for strangers to make suggestions as to how a prominent local resident might employ his funds and quite another to have such suggestions backed by substantial and respected peers and businessmen. After all, Polk Pilchard is out, at least in part, to gain the admiration of his fellow Durginites, and where better to start than with you two gentlemen?"

"Es verdad," Callahan said. *"Señor Barnet y migo, somos hombres de mucho respetabilidad aquí."*

All settled, Faro thought. Except, of course, for the fact that Polk Pilchard wants to see what our tripes look like in the daylight, because of us giving his wife what he can't or don't care to. He looked at his watch: a little after two. Polk Pilchard should be finished with his lunch with the Ginn sisters about now, and it wouldn't be out of the way for him to drop in at Callahan's after. He patted his vest, reassuring himself that the Reid's, retrieved from Turkey Nickerson's hideout, was there, and regretted that he had not thought to bring along the shotgun.

"That heat with the horse yesterday, that was impressive," Barnet said. "Gave everybody a taste of what the races you're trying to set up will be like. You had many orders for cycles out of that, Major?"

"I, ah, have had other pressing affairs to attend to since that time," Doc said. Until the legal formalities were settled, he had decided to say nothing of his and Faro's role in the capture of Turkey Nickerson and Ben and Mike. It would cause a lot of confusion right now, he felt, explaining just what Major Hilary Mordaunt was doing embroiled with such characters. By the time it all came out, he was sure that he could come up with a story that would work to his advantage.

"Well, I guess you could dispose of the dozen you've got and send off to Massachusetts for more," Barnet said. "I had two women in this morning, asking if there were cycling skirts made, like the divided ones for horseback."

"There are ladies' bicycles, designed to accommodate the traditional and flattering garments of the fair sex," Doc said. "Special costumes are not required for this healthful sport."

"All the same, it wouldn't do my Matilda any harm to run up a few numbers she could call cycling skirts and let me have the selling of them," Barnet said. "In my experience, once there's a craze going, you can't have too much stuff connected with it for sale—it'll all go, even the trash. Wish I had the selling of your cycles, Major—I'd have 'em gone in no time, and orders wired in for delivery by fast freight."

"I appreciate your interest, Barnet," Doc said, "but you'll understand that as the local Macduff's representative, I am not open to side arrangements."

"Well, sure," Barnet said. "Hey, here comes Polk Pilchard."

Doc and Faro both rose from their seats as Pilchard entered Callahan's, with Faro's left hand drifting close to his vest. Pilchard bore no visible arms, but the fit of his clothes was such that about anything, up to the size of an ax handle, could have been easily concealed.

"Major, Blake," he said curtly, but without overt rage. Faro relaxed his tensed hand. "Like a word with you. Callahan, bring these gentlemen and me a bottle of rye over to that back table, and three glasses." Faro's preference, as always, was for bourbon, but rye would do; the main thing was that Pilchard seemed prepared to be sensible. Maybe Doc's strategy had something to recommend it, after all. With Barnet's and Callahan's backing, it could be that the cycle race and the super poker game would come off.

"Been studying it out," Pilchard said when they were seated and drinking. "That despoiling stuff. 'Melia got at the wine again this morning and talked some more. 'Pears to me that you men are the latest, that's all, not the main ones. I don't care for it, not one bit, but I don't feel it's a killing matter any more, and I am working out just what kind of damn I give about it. Anyhow, it seems to have come out that I got to feel grateful to you, some ways—wasn't that I'd followed you out to the Good Indian, I'd never have got it back, and that'll make Polk Pilchard a name that Durgin'll have to reckon with up into the nineties, I'd say."

"So you worked out your business arrangements with the Ginn sisters to all-around satisfaction?" Doc said.

Polk Pilchard nodded. "Mine, anyhow. I figured it out, what a vein like that could mean, and offered them about a tenth of what the takings would have to be. Not an unfair deal, as they won't have the trouble of seeing to it, and, anyhow, it was only inherited property to them, nothing they'd had to work for."

Doc's effort to restrain his opinion of Polk Pilchard's business acumen was visible to Faro. "Ah, then," he said after a moment. "With everything running your way, and previous circumstances overlooked, I believe that Mr. Blake and I may take it that the bicycle race, with its generous trophy contributed by your good self, and the grand gathering of gamesters proposed by Mr. Blake will go forward under your sponsorship?"

Pilchard shook his head. "Nope. Not just now, anyhow. When I get the Good Indian producing again, I expect so, but it's taken about all I have ready to hand to buy those girls out. They struck a damned hard bargain, but it was worth it to me to have the mine all to myself. So"—Pilchard rose from his chair and looked at them—"I can't say I'll ever like you fellows, but I got to admit that you done me some kind of good turn. You're welcome to the rest of the bottle."

Pilchard paused to exchange a word with Callahan on his way out of the saloon, and Faro said, "Bet you what you like he's telling Porfirio that we'll pay."

"I won't take that one," Doc said. "It really irks me that that skinflint is going to come out ahead on that mine deal, even if he has had to give the girls a big chunk of cash for it."

"What irks me, if irk is what I think it is," Faro said, "is that we put in a lot of time here, and it don't look like there's to be anything to show for it, barring me becoming cycle champeen of Durgin."

"Ah, yes," Doc said. "Glad you brought that up." He called to Barnet, who came over to the table and sat down. "Barnet, old chap, how would you like to become the Durgin representative for Macduff's incomparable cycles?"

Faro looked out at the landscape, broken now as it rose to the high plateau and reddened in the light of the sunset into which the train bore them. "That is about the fastest I ever got out of a town without that the law was chasing me," he said.

Doc, seated next to him, shrugged. "Nothing to stay for. Barnet gave me a fair price for the bicycles, the races and the game were off, and no immediate chance of hitting Pilchard up for investing in Macduff, or at least thinking he was doing that. The only thing Durgin had to offer was the prospect of hanging around to testify against Nickerson and his cloddish henchmen, quite possibly to our embarrassment. They may be turned loose, but that's not our affair, my boy—we're not in the business of being public-spirited."

He looked out at the wind-and-water-sculptured shapes that dominated the view from the window and said, "Once you've done what you can and found out what you can't in a place, the thing to do is move on and hope for the luck of a train out in a little while, the way we had. Two changes, no more, and a couple of days and we'll be in the Bay City, ready for new endeavors. If they haven't thought of it already, I might try to work up a cycle race down Telegraph Hill. With that grade, there'd be almost sure to be a fatality or so, and there's nothing like the hope of that for drawing a crowd."

"And there is always fellows staying at the Palace that is good for bigger games than Polk Pilchard could ever get geared up for," Faro said. "Hey, Doc, I guess we ain't lost that much over this Durgin business, after all."

"The best way to look at it," Doc said. "If we didn't,

we'd have a hell of a hard time convincing ourselves that we're living any kind of life a man could stand, wouldn't we?" He settled himself back in his seat, tipped his hat over his face and drifted off to sleep.

Faro looked out the window at the landscape as it deepened in hue, the distant mesas and ragged lines of arroyos taking on tinges of purple and deep rose along with the prevailing brown-pink. After a while he realized that he had not eaten since breakfast at Mrs. Pyle's that morning and that his stomach was rumbling. There was a dining car ahead, he remembered, and he got up, savoring in advance whatever it might offer. Hotels, boardinghouses, lunch counters, they all offered food that was welcome to a hungry man, but for the real pleasures of eating, he had never found anything quite equal to a good railroad dining car.

"If you don't mind sharing a table, sir?" the waiter who greeted him said. "None empty just now."

"Sure thing," Faro said. "I'll rub elbows with any fellow traveler who'll have me."

"Fine, sir. This way, please."

The waiter led him to a table occupied by two women dressed in identical traveling dresses, and bent to address one of them. "Of course," she said, looking up. "Oh—well, do sit down, Mr. Blake."

Evidently Juniper and Geneva Ginn had decided to leave Durgin about as impulsively as Faro and Doc. And, Faro wondered, just which the hell one is that talking to me?

Chapter 16

The dinner was as good as Faro had expected, and it was a treat to him to have what he ordered slid deftly in front of him instead of having to stab for it in a platter in the center of the table, maneuvering around the other boarders for a choice bit.

Juniper and Geneva Ginn, he noted, now ate only normal amounts of food. Well, it must have been a strain on two healthy girls, trying to get by on board that was supposedly being given only to one.

"Seems to me you left Durgin pretty quick," Faro said.

"So did you," said Juniper, the one seated next to him, he was pretty sure.

"Well, my business was done with," Faro said.

"So was ours," Geneva, across from him (or just maybe Juniper), said. "We saw that Polk Pilchard at lunch, and he made us an offer for our deed to the

155

Good Indian, and we took it, and he went back to his house and got the money he'd said he would, and gave it to us, and we came on our way."

"I hope," Faro said, "that he didn't get it on the cheap. A mine with a vein of gold like that one, that's something it don't do to let go of for less'n top dollar."

"I think we got top dollar for the Good Indian, Mr. Blake," Juniper (almost certainly) said. "Junie, what do you . . ." So that was Geneva, after all.

"Why not, Gen?"

Geneva Ginn turned to Faro and said, "Mr. Blake, are you an honest man? I mean, really an honest one, the kind that'd go running to the police if he heard of something unlawful or dishonest someone had done?"

"Was I like that, I'd be wore down to a stump with dropping in on the law folks," Faro said. "Bad enough worrying about what low-thinking people does to me and my friends without taking care for the population in general."

"I thought so," Juniper Ginn said. "Well, I guess we're a little like that, too. So I guess we don't have to worry if we tell you."

Faro listened, fascinated, as the sisters told the last chapter in the saga of the Good Indian mine. The key factor was the single ingot of pure gold that Uncle Norris had retained as a souvenir of the mine's bonanza days.

"We always loved to touch it when we went to visit him," Geneva said. "It wasn't very big, about the size of a big bar of chocolate, but it was so heavy, so soft to touch, and it felt so nice in our hands. Well, when Uncle Norris died and we took over the place, we searched that out first of all. And we kept it with us always, one of us carrying it wherever we went."

"So it was with us when we were in San Francisco," Juniper said, "when that Nickerson man burned the house down. And of course we took it with us when we went to Durgin. And when I rode out to the mine, I took it along with me, 'cause it fit right in my hand, and I thought I could use it to hit a snake or something that might come along there, seeing as neither of us had a gun or anything."

"Oh, Lordy," Faro said. "So when you . . ."

"When Gen came in and hit that Nickerson and they untied me, I saw Pilchard was there, and it came to me. I slipped out for a minute, and I rubbed the gold onto the broken rock where I'd been and onto the ropes I'd been tied with. It used up about half the bar, but that's all the gold there is in the Good Indian."

"If Polk Pilchard hadn't been so anxious to get through the business fast, thinking he was cheating us," Geneva said, "he'd likely have done a proper inspection. But I think he was afraid we'd see how big the vein was and wouldn't sell to him."

"I got to congratulate you," Faro said, after a moment of admiration for the twins' native talent for high larceny. Put them in partnership with Doc Prentiss and they could round up most of the loose money west of the Mississippi. He looked at his watch. "Best be getting on back to my coach and see can I settle myself in for slumber. All the years I been traveling, seems I never get it worked out so's I can get a good night's sleep sitting up in the cars. You ladies find the same thing?"

"Oh," Geneva Ginn said. "Junie and me, we don't have to worry about that, this trip. What with the money from Polk Pilchard, and knowing that we won't have any trouble about the fire insurance now that that Nickerson's in jail and they can prove it on him, we're feeling pretty well fixed, and we decided to go back home in style, hired our own private car."

"Real beds, really soft ones, not like Pullman berths.

And a bathroom with a big tub . . ." Juniper Ginn said, looking dreamily at Faro.

"All to ourselves," Geneva Ginn said.

"Thass nice for you, you being twins and all," Faro said huskily. He took his glass and drank the last of the wine he had ordered for dinner.

"Oh, yes," Juniper Ginn said, "it is nice, just the two of us. But we're together so much, we do sort of get talked out sometimes. We play card games, but then we can get tired of that."

"There's things we don't get tired of, though," Geneva Ginn said.

"I believe I . . . ah," Faro said, "recollect some sort of un-tired times with you ladies, back at Ma Pyle's."

"So do we." Each twin spoke at the same time, then snorted with laughter.

"It was grand fun, drying off, and then after," Juniper Ginn said.

"It was such a comfort, it about saved my wits when I was so scared for Junie," Geneva Ginn said.

"Well, uh, I am glad to hear it," Faro said. He looked at the identical smiling faces. "It would be an almighty pleasure to me if we was to come to getting at more of the same."

"Oh, yes," Geneva said. "But not separately this time. Junie and me, we like to do most things together."

"Ah, isn't that nice, Junie?" Geneva said. Faro's left hand was squeezing one of her breasts and his right one of Juniper's as he moved atop her.

"Oh, it is, Gen." Juniper clamped her legs around him; Geneva moved closer and ran her tongue into his ear, then sent her hand down his back, stroking and fondling. She gripped him just short of the point of inflicting pain, and the strong but gentle pressure brought him to climax; her sister gasped and shuddered under him.

"Nice, sister, oh yes, how nice," Juniper said.

"Mmm, I felt it too," Geneva said.

Faro, after half an hour in the private car with the twins, was feeling distinctly lightheaded and not at all sure whether he was on a train or at sea or aloft in a hot-air balloon. After what he had just been through with Juniper, it didn't seem that there was much left of him, but he was somehow sure that there was. "Turkey Nickerson used to say that fair shares all around was his motto," he said, "and, while he ain't a man I could cotton to, I will say that he has the right of it there. Miss Geneva, you care to see if you and me can get up to what me and Miss Juniper was just at?"

"Oh, yes," the twins said in unison. Juniper wriggled from under him, and he turned to receive Geneva, while Juniper looked on with a wide, lax smile. He slid into Geneva easily and reached for Juniper, fingers moving over and into where he had just been.

The sky outside the day coach windows was just changing from black to pearl gray when Faro stumbled up the aisle and fell into the seat beside Doc, breathing deeply.

Doc stirred and pushed his hat brim up. "Seems you took a long time for dinner," he said.

Faro composed himself for sleep as best he could on the seat, so much harder than the twins' plump mattresses—and a good bit harder than the twins themselves.

"Well, Doc," he said, "there was one hell of a dessert."